The Missing Puppy

and other tales

The Missing Puppy

and other tales

by Holly Webb

Illustrated by Sophy Williams

tiger tales

tiger tales

5 River Road, Suite 128, Wilton, CT 06897
Published in the United States 2016
Text copyright © Holly Webb
The Missing Puppy originally published as
Max the Missing Puppy 2008
The Homeless Puppy originally published as
Harry the Homeless Puppy 2009
The Runaway Puppy originally published as
Buttons the Runaway Puppy 2009
Illustrations copyright © Sophy Williams
The Missing Puppy originally published as
Max the Missing Puppy 2008
The Homeless Puppy originally published as
Harry the Homeless Puppy 2009
The Runaway Puppy originally published as
Buttons the Runaway Puppy 2009
ISBN-13: 978-1-68010-404-2
ISBN-10: 1-68010-404-7
Printed in China
STP/1000/0164/0917
10 9 8 7 6 5

For more insight and activities, visit us at www.tigertalesbooks.com

Contents

The
Missing
Puppy

Contents

For Rosie

Chapter One
A Dream Come True

Molly opened the gate, and stood holding it, waiting impatiently for her parents to catch up. "This is it!" she called. "Number 42!" She was sure she could hear squeaking and yapping from inside the house, and she couldn't wait to get inside.

At last her parents caught up. "Go and ring the bell, then!" said Molly's dad.

Molly heard the bell chime inside the house, and it was followed by an explosion of deep woofs. Then she heard paws thudding, and claws clicking, and something thumped into the door. Molly jumped back in surprise.

"Jackson, move! How can I open the door with you in front of it?" The voice didn't sound angry, more as though the dog's owner was trying not to laugh. "And the rest of you aren't helping!"

The deep barking had now been joined by a lot of squeaky little noises, all sounding very excited. The door opened, and a friendly-looking woman attempted to hold back a tide of black-and-white puppies as they swarmed around her feet. A huge, gray, shaggy dog was sitting beside her.

"Oh, good, you shut the gate. The puppies are a bit excited, I'm afraid, and they're desperate to get out and explore. I'm Sally Hughes, we spoke on the phone. Come on in!"

"I'm James Martin," Molly's dad said, picking up a puppy who'd managed to scramble over Mrs. Hughes's foot. "You spoke to my wife, Claire, on the phone, and this is our daughter, Molly. The dog-crazy one!"

They followed the excited puppies into the house. Molly looked at them in amazement. Mrs. Hughes had told her mom that there were six puppies, but surely there were more here. They seemed to be everywhere!

Mrs. Hughes led everyone into the kitchen. Another massive dog was stretched out, dozing on a comfy-looking cushion in the corner. Molly was sure she heard her groan as the puppies flooded back in and threw themselves all over her.

Mrs. Hughes smiled. "Poor Lady! I think she's actually looking forward to the puppies going to new homes. They're wearing her out!" She put cups of coffee down in front of Molly's mom and dad, and poured Molly a glass of juice.

Molly sipped from her glass, perched on the edge of her chair, wishing she could go and play with the puppies who were bouncing on their mom.

Mrs. Hughes noticed her hopeful eyes. "Go ahead and play with them! Just watch out for the puppies' dad,

Jackson. He's completely friendly, but he's huge, and if he wants to join in he can knock you over without meaning to!"

Molly knelt down on the floor, and the puppies looked at her with interest. The bravest of them started to creep slowly over to her, tail wagging gently. Molly stretched out a hand hopefully, and he butted it with his soft little head, then darted back. Molly thought he looked almost as though he was giggling!

"Mrs. Hughes?" she asked. "Why don't the puppies look like Jackson and Lady? They've got short fur, and they're black-and-white, but their parents are gray."

"That's the way it is with Old English sheepdogs," Mrs. Hughes said.

"They're born with that short, springy, black-and-white fur, and when it grows longer, it gets much lighter."

Dad was looking at Lady, her long fur glossy and smooth as it trailed over her cushion. "Grooming is going to be a lot of work."

Mrs. Hughes nodded seriously. "Yes, it really is. You have to make sure their coats are clean, and that they don't have any sore spots under all that fur. And they need a *lot* of exercise. Old English sheepdogs are a big commitment. I mean, no dogs are easy to take care of, but these can be hard work."

Molly looked up at her parents. It sounded scary, but she still wanted to take one of the puppies home!

Her mom looked doubtful. "Maybe this isn't a good idea since we've never had a dog before. Maybe a smaller dog would be better...."

The bravest puppy, who had a mostly white face, cute black ears, and a pirate-style eye patch, was creeping up to Molly again. This time he jumped up so his paws were on her lap, and he gave her a quick little lick.

Molly gasped delightedly. She'd been listening to her mom and hadn't noticed him. She tickled him under the chin. "I don't mind hard work," she said earnestly.

Another puppy, who had just the same adorable pirate look, bounded over and jumped into Molly's lap. Then he sat with his tongue hanging out, looking very pleased with himself.

Mrs. Hughes smiled. "It's not all work. They're incredibly affectionate dogs, and very good with children. Your daughter will have a friend for life." She crouched down next to Molly. "Those two are the boy puppies. They get into everything. The girls are a little bit more shy."

But now that their brothers had proven that this girl wasn't scary, the other puppies came crowding around to be petted, too. Soon Molly was covered in a black-and-white puppy blanket. She saw Lady watching her, one big dark eye peering out from behind her beautiful long fringe. The big dog sighed happily, and Molly was sure she was glad that someone else was being climbed on for once.

Molly's parents had been talking quietly. Molly tried to listen, but the puppies kept licking her ears, which made it difficult to hear. She hoped they hadn't changed their minds! When they'd seen the ad in the paper saying *Puppies for Sale*, and read that the house was only half an hour's drive away, it had seemed so perfect. It had taken forever to convince Mom and Dad that she was old enough to have a dog. They'd been saying "When you're older" for years! Molly didn't think she could bear it if she had to wait any longer. These puppies were so adorable. Molly could just imagine running along the beach after school every day with a huge, silver-furred dog like Jackson galloping beside her.

At last Dad came over and squatted down next to the puppies, too. Molly and all the puppies stared at him. Then one of the bouncy boy puppies leaned over and nudged him with his furry head, looking at him with

21

twinkly, dark eyes.

Dad gently picked up the puppy and smiled at Molly. "So, do you think you can manage to keep one of these little rascals exercised?" he asked.

Molly gasped in delight. "You mean yes? We can have one?" She wrapped her arms around the other boy puppy, who was trying to burrow under her shirt.

"Yes. But you'll have to take care of the puppy, Molly. And it won't be a puppy for that long, either—soon it will be a great big dog the size of Lady and Jackson over there." Dad tickled the puppy, who wriggled happily. Then he looked down at the puppies romping all around them. "Now we just have to choose one...."

One!

Molly knew she should be excited about having a puppy at all, but she hadn't imagined how difficult it would be to pick just one. The puppies were all so sweet, and she wanted to take all of them home! How could she choose one—when it meant leaving all the others behind?

The two boys were fighting over a chew-toy now, pulling it back and forth with pretend fierce growls. The fight looked even funnier because they were so alike, the same size and with almost identical markings. The only noticeable difference was that their eye patches were on the opposite eyes—sitting side by side, they were like mirror images.

"You like them, don't you, Molly?" Mom asked, watching and laughing as one of the puppies let go, leaving his brother rolling onto his bottom, still clutching the toy. "Should we take one of the boys?"

"Oh, yes, they're really sweet. But how are we going to choose just one of them?" Molly stretched out her fingers to the puppies, who came over at once to sniff and lick them. She tickled the puppies behind their ears and hugged them as they climbed up into her lap. "Couldn't we…?"

"Only one puppy, Molly!" Mom said firmly. "One dog is quite enough."

Dad was nodding, too, and Molly sighed and looked at the puppies. Just then, the puppy with the right eye patch went to join his sisters, who were taking turns hanging off their mom's ears.

The other puppy watched them for a minute, then turned and gazed up at Molly, his tongue hanging out a bit so he looked goofy. Molly giggled. "Okay," she said, lifting him gently under his front legs, and snuggling him up against her shoulder. "Please can we have this one? He's really friendly and cuddly."

Mom leaned over to pet him. "He definitely is adorable. What are we going to call him?"

Molly gave the puppy a thoughtful look as he slobbered into her shoulder. "I think we should call him Max!"

Chapter Two
Best of Friends

A week later, Molly and her parents were able to take Max home. He was eight weeks old now, and ready to leave his mother. Two of his sisters were about to go to new homes, too, and Mrs. Hughes said she was sure the others would find owners soon.

Molly still wished they could have Max's brother as well; they were such a pair that Molly hated to split them up. Then Max spotted Molly, flung himself at her, and nearly knocked her over, and Molly thought that maybe *two* dogs doing that all the time might be a bit much. But she was so happy that he remembered her!

"Hmmm. We're going to have to take him to a good puppy-training class," Molly's mom said. "It won't be long before he's big enough to hurt someone by accident. We need to be able to get him to calm down."

Mrs. Hughes was nodding. "I can recommend a local trainer. Max has just had his first shots, so you can take him to classes in a couple of weeks when he's had the second set. It's good to start young."

It was very exciting taking Max home. Mom and Dad had already spent quite a while putting a dog gate in the back of the car so that Max had his own special place to ride. Mom had to keep telling Molly to sit still, as she just couldn't help twisting around in her seat to check that Max was okay, all on his own back there.

At the house there was his new basket, his food bowl, and his leash for walks. Mrs. Hughes had said to introduce him to outdoor walks gently, as he was only used to quick runs in her garden. Molly was really looking forward to taking him for walks on the beach, but they needed to wait until after Max's booster vaccinations.

Meanwhile, Max was enjoying settling in at his new home. He did miss his brother and sisters, but Molly was a new and interesting person to play with, and he had her all to himself. He didn't have to share his toys either, and there were plenty! Molly had spent all her money on tennis balls and a nylon bone that would be good for Max's new teeth. They had a wonderful afternoon playing games. Max ran around so much he fell asleep in the middle of a game that they'd invented. All of a sudden, he had stopped bouncing, and when Molly had peered worriedly under the blanket to check that he was all

right, she had found him stretched
out with his nose between his paws,
fast asleep.

Molly had begged for Max to be allowed to sleep in her room, but Mom and Dad said no. They knew Max would end up on Molly's bed and not in his basket, even though Molly promised he wouldn't. "It's nice having a puppy on your bed, Molly," Mom explained, "but once Max is his full size, there'd be no room in your bed for you! You can't let him get on your bed now and then change your mind when he's bigger. He wouldn't understand."

So Max had to stay downstairs. Molly had given him her old teddy bear to snuggle up to, and a hot-water bottle, so he'd feel like he was curled up next to his mom, but it wasn't the same. After all the cuddles, Max just didn't understand why he was suddenly all on his own. He yapped hopefully, expecting someone to come back and play with him, but no one came. He got up, and pattered around the kitchen sniffing, trying to figure out where they all were. Earlier, Molly had played a game where she popped out from behind chairs at him—maybe this was the same? But she wasn't behind any of the chairs.

Max trailed back to his basket with his tail hanging sadly. Where had they all gone? Were they going to come back? He snuffled and whimpered to himself for a little while, then the exhausting day caught up with him again, and he fell asleep, burrowed into his blanket.

Upstairs Molly listened worriedly. It was so horrible hearing him cry, but Mom and Dad had explained that it would only upset Max more if she went down and then left him again. Her bedroom door was open, and she could hear the noises from the kitchen. She crept out very quietly, and leaned over the banister. He sounded so sad! But he was definitely getting quieter, so maybe he was going to sleep. Molly was tired, too, so she sat down on the top step, leaning against the wall, and tried not to let her eyes close.

Molly's parents had been watching TV in the living room. When they came upstairs a couple of hours later, Molly was fast asleep on the top step.

"Max…," she muttered sleepily, as her dad picked her up.

"He's fast asleep in his basket, Molly. Don't worry. Go to sleep."

The weekend just flew by. At school on Monday, everyone was envious when Molly told them about Max. She had a couple of photos that Dad had printed out for her, and she showed them off proudly.

"Oh, he's beautiful, Molly! My brother has an Old English sheepdog. They make great pets." Mrs. Ford, Molly's teacher, looked at the photo admiringly in the playground before school. "You should show those to the class when we do weekend news."

Molly didn't normally like the class news sessions that much, as she never felt like she had anything very exciting to say! But today she couldn't wait to tell everyone about her puppy. It was nice to have them all admiring Max's picture, too, because she was really missing him. She couldn't help wondering what he was doing, and if he was missing her, too. Mom had promised to play with Max, but she'd be busy doing stuff on the computer, too, as she worked from home. Molly hoped Mom wouldn't get too busy and forget about him.

Molly's school was really close to her house, so she walked there with her mom, and they picked up her friend Amy on the way. Then Amy's mom brought them home. That Monday Molly hurried Amy all the way back to their road, and then she raced home and flung herself through the front door.

Max jumped up and shot out of the kitchen to greet her. He'd been curled up in his basket, half-dozing, and wishing someone would play with him. He loved his new house, but it got very quiet without Molly there. Molly's mom had tried her best, but she just wasn't the same. With Molly he didn't have to stand there holding his bone and looking hopeful; she *knew* when he wanted to play. He danced around her, barking excitedly. When she swept him up for a hug he did his best to lick her all over, wanting her to know how much he'd longed for her to come home.

"Ooooh, stop, Max, not my ears! You're really tickling!" Molly held him out at arm's length and laughed at him.

"I don't need a bath. Did you have a nice day? Was he okay, Mom? Did he behave himself?"

Her mom was leaning on the doorframe and laughing. "Yes, but I think he really missed you. He looked all around the house several times, and he sat by the front door for quite a while. Why don't you take him in the yard? I took him out quickly at lunchtime, but I'm sure he'd like to go out again."

Max seemed to understand what "yard" meant. He dashed to the door, and jumped up and down, squeaking.

Molly giggled. "No, I think I need a rest after school … it's okay, Max, I'm teasing! Come on, silly." She grabbed his squeaky ball and opened the door, letting Max streak out in a black-and-white blur.

He loved to be outside!

Max didn't stop missing Molly while she was at school—and she seemed to have to go to school all the time! He spent lots of time sniffing around for her, and he figured out that he could sneakily climb on to the back of the sofa to look out the window and see if she was coming. He got in trouble if Molly's mom caught him doing that, though.

Max was sure that if he could get outside, he could find Molly and be with her. He knew she missed him, too, and didn't understand why she went out without him. It had only taken him a few days of being in the house without her to explore everywhere inside. By the fifth day of Molly being at school, Max was very bored.

"We'll do lots of playing in the yard this weekend, Max," Molly promised as she got ready to leave for school on Friday morning. "I really wish we could go on the beach and show you the ocean, but Mrs. Hughes said you'll have to wait until about a week after your second vaccinations."

"He'd probably only try and eat the sand," Mom said, looking at Max's food bowl. It was empty, as usual, and polished sparkly-clean. "That dog is always hungry." She scratched him under the chin to show she wasn't really angry, and Max closed his eyes happily. Under the chin was his absolute favorite place to be tickled, and Mom and Molly sounded happy and excited. Everything was good.

Except Molly was about to go! Not again. Max gave a mournful little howl.

"I know, I'm sorry. But I'll be back this afternoon, and then we've got the whole weekend. And it's vacation! I'd almost forgotten! Nine days of no school. We'll spend lots of time outside. It's going to be great." Molly kissed the top of his head, and followed Mom outside, leaving Max staring sadly at the door.

Molly's mom was very busy that day. She kept shooing Max away when he tried to play. She did take him for a couple of little runs in the yard, but she wanted to go back in long before he did. By the middle of the afternoon, Max was missing Molly. It was a hot, sleepy day, even though it was only May, and being stuck in the house was making Max restless. Maybe Molly's mom was ready to play again. He brought his squeaky bone to her for a game, but she said, "Not now, Max," in a really firm voice, so he went and lay down in his basket, feeling bored. He rested his chin on the edge of the basket and sighed.

Maybe he should just sleep, and see if Molly's mom wanted to play later. His eyes were slowly closing when something fluttered past his nose. Max opened one eye to see a large butterfly swooping around his head. Surprised, he jumped up and barked furiously. What was it?

Mom dashed in, looking worried. Then she laughed. "Oh, Max, it's all right, it's only a butterfly. We'll get him out. You've probably never seen one before."

The butterfly was in no hurry to leave. Mom tried to waft it toward the kitchen window where it had come in, but it fluttered off into the living room and eventually settled on the curtains. Mom opened the window and after a couple of failed attempts, she scooped it out with a magazine.

"There," she said, soothingly, putting the magazine back on the coffee table. "It's gone now. Oh, look, Molly will be home soon. I need to finish that last little bit of work." She went back to the computer in her office down the hall.

Max pricked up his ears when Mom mentioned Molly. Was she coming? He looked hopefully at the front door, but no Molly appeared. Disappointed, he wandered back into the living room and scrambled up on to the sofa so that he could look out the window and wait for her.

Then he noticed that Mom had left the window open.

Max jumped up, and stuck his head out the window, his nose quivering with excitement.

Now he could go and find Molly!

Molly dashed down the road from Amy's house, calling a quick good-bye over her shoulder. She went in the front door, expecting Max to be there leaping around her feet. But the house was strangely quiet. Max must be asleep.

Molly headed quietly into the kitchen, not wanting to wake him. He was so cute when he was asleep. Max's basket was empty, and she looked around, confused. Maybe he was with Mom in her office?

Feeling a little anxious, Molly walked quickly back into the hallway and opened the office door.

Her mom looked up with a start. "Molly! I'm sorry, I didn't hear you. I've been desperately trying to get this finished before the holiday. Did you have a nice day?"

"Yes—but Mom, where's Max?"

Mom looked down at Molly's feet as though she expected to see Max there. "Isn't he in his basket? I thought he was sleeping."

"No, I can't find him anywhere," Molly said. "He always comes running when I get home from school."

"He probably got himself shut in somewhere," said Mom, but she didn't sound as sure as Molly would have liked. She got up and together they went through every room in the house, calling to Max. Every time they opened a door, Molly hoped she'd hear a little patter of paws, and wild yapping, but there was nothing.

No Max.

They went back through every room, urgently this time, searching under all the beds in case he'd gotten himself stuck, opening cupboards, Molly frantically calling.

Still nothing.

Back downstairs, Mom was starting to look really worried, too. She stood in the living room, trying to think. "I took him in the yard after lunch, but he definitely came back in with me. Then I was working.... Oh! that butterfly surprised him. It flew in through the kitchen window," she explained. "He didn't know what it was. I let it out the window in here...." She did a slow turn toward the window, and her hand went to her mouth in horror. The window was still propped open. Definitely wide enough for a little dog to fit through.

Chapter Three
Max in Danger

Meanwhile, Max was trotting along the pavement, sniffing enthusiastically. He knew he could find Molly. He'd know her smell anywhere! He had wriggled out the window quite easily, and fallen into the flower bed, but it didn't matter. Molly was going to be so pleased to see him! Only—he had been expecting to find her by now.

Molly's house was on the edge of the town, and although Max didn't know it, he was going completely the wrong way, heading out of town and away from the school where Molly had been. He had taken a few turns that looked interesting, passing some more houses like Molly's. Instinctively he'd avoided crossing any roads. The town was very quiet, but a few cars did come past, and he'd been scared. He shrank back against the fences and hedges as he heard the cars coming, roaring things that he sensed were dangerous. He kept hidden against the hedges, and no one saw him. Now he was heading along the road that led to Springfield, a small town several miles away. It was so nice to be

53

outside, and he trotted along happily for a while, covering a big distance for such a small dog. He would see Molly soon, he was sure.

Eventually he came across an interesting-looking sloping path leading off the pavement. It was rough and stony, with sweet-smelling plants on either side. Max plunged down, eager to explore. The path led gently down to a beach, not the main beach where all the vacationers came, but a small rocky cove without much sand that was cut off at high tide. Max stopped short as he got his first sight of the ocean. The waves made a swooshing sound as they rushed in and out over the pebbles. He had a feeling that this wasn't where he'd find Molly, but it looked so exciting that he had to go and investigate.

He skittered down the rest of the path, scrambling over the stones, and stood on the beach, sniffing the salty smell of the ocean. It moved, and made a noise—was it alive? He went closer, ears pricked, ready to run if he needed to. Suddenly, a wave swept in and soaked his paws. Max yelped and jumped backward. It was cold!

Max stood back from the water and barked angrily at the ocean. It didn't seem to be listening, just sweeping in again and hissing at his feet. Max looked at it with his head to one side. Maybe it was playing a game. Perhaps it wanted him to chase it? He tried, dashing forward as the waves rolled back, then yapping excitedly as it chased him. It was a great game! And the ocean didn't get tired and say it needed to sit down, like Molly and her mom. Max played for a long time.

Then a chilly wind blew up, ruffling the surface of the ocean, and Max shivered. Suddenly, he realized how hungry he was. Molly would be home by now, and wondering where he was. Max whirled around and scrambled back up the path as quickly as he could. But when he got to the top, he looked around. Which way was home from here? He couldn't remember which way he'd come—he hadn't been thinking about having to go *back*.

Anxiously, Max sniffed the air, hoping to pick up a familiar smell to tell him which way to go. Nothing. No smell of home, or Molly. Max sat down at the top of the path, huddling close to the sign that said *To the Ocean*.

No one was around; just empty road stretching out in both directions. Seagulls were crying, but that was the only sound. Max whined miserably. He was lost.

Suddenly, a low buzzing sound rose in the distance, quickly getting louder. Max looked around, and cowered back against the sign as a car shot by, engine roaring, and vanished down the road. He had to

move. He needed to find Molly, and get away from noisy monsters like that. Determined, he trotted a few steps down the road. He wasn't sure if it was the right way, but he had to go *somewhere*.

The road seemed to go on forever. Max was starving—he was used to several small meals of his special puppy food every day, and it felt like he'd missed at least three of them.

As he continued on, his paws started to hurt, too, because he'd never walked so far before. And it was getting harder to see, the daylight leaving a strange half-dusk that made shapes loom up at him. All the trees seemed to be waving big, scary branches at him, and the seagulls' cries suddenly sounded eerie.

Max stopped to rest, hiding in between some clumps of grass at the side of the road. He'd gone a long way out of town by now, and the road didn't have pavement anymore, just grassy banks on either side. Things were scurrying in the hedges behind him, and more and more Max wished he'd never left his warm, comfortable, *safe* house behind.

He pushed on, determined to find his way home. It suddenly seemed to have gotten much darker, and Max was so tired and confused that he started to wander along in the middle of the road, his legs shaking with weariness. But he refused to give up.

Another low buzzing noise; this time he felt it in his paws before he heard it. A car! Max looked around, frightened and confused by the bright lights that were racing up behind him. He tried to get out of the way, but he didn't know which way to go, and he wavered disastrously in its path. The driver didn't even see him.

The car caught him with the edge of its front bumper, and Max was thrown clear, landing in the hedges. He lay unconscious in the long grass, his leg bleeding.

When Molly's dad got home from work, the house was empty, but he could hear Molly's voice calling from the yard.

"Max! Max, where are you?" Molly sounded upset, and her dad dropped his bag in the hall and hurried out to see what was going on.

"Did Max get out?" he asked anxiously. "He didn't wriggle under the fence, did he? I thought that gap was too small."

Molly shook her head. Her eyes were

full of tears, and she gave her dad a hug, burying her face in his coat. She didn't want to be the one to tell him.

Molly's mom came down the side path around the house. "Oh, James, you're back!" She was feeling so guilty about accidentally letting Max out, and she kept telling Molly how sorry she was. "I left the front window open, and Max got out. We've been up and down the street, but we can't find him anywhere."

Molly was trying hard to forgive her mom, because she knew she hadn't meant to leave the window open, but it was difficult.

"There's just no sign of him," Mom said, close to tears. "I've spoken to all the neighbors, and no one has seen him.

63

But they've all promised to keep an eye out for him."

"If only he'd had his collar on," Molly said miserably. They'd bought Max a collar, but he hadn't been wearing it. He hadn't needed it on when he was only in the house and yard. They'd also been planning to take Max to the vet to get his next vaccinations, and the vet was going to put a microchip in his neck. It would have meant that if he got lost, any vet could check the chip and would know who he belonged to. They'd made an appointment for it to be done next week. They were taking him to the vet where Mrs. Hughes brought her dogs. It was a half-hour drive away, but Mrs. Hughes had said they were really good. The thought made Molly's eyes fill with tears. Who knew where Max would be by then?

That night, Molly went to bed worn out from searching up and down her street, and around the town, and cried herself to sleep. But a hundred miles away, another girl lay awake, too excited to close her eyes. In the corner of Jasmine's bedroom was a small suitcase, already packed. She knew she should go to sleep, since they were going to get up at six, and Dad wanted to be on the road by six-thirty, but she just couldn't stop thinking about how exciting it was to be going on vacation. And to the beach! It was only May, so it wouldn't be very hot, but she could put her feet in the water, and build sandcastles, and eat tons and tons of ice cream! It was going to be fantastic.

Jasmine must have fallen asleep eventually, because the next thing she knew, her mom was shaking her awake. For once she didn't have to be told to get up quickly; she was downstairs five minutes later.

"I'm too excited for breakfast," said Jasmine, when her mother offered toast.

"You need to eat something. It's going to take us all morning to get there," her dad said. He was drinking a cup of coffee and looking at the map.

"Okay. So we get off the highway, and then once we get to Springfield, the nearest town, we keep going along the cliff road, but we have to make sure we watch for the sign for the cottage. The cottage owners said that if we get to Athens, a town about five miles further on, then we have to turn around because we've missed it! Okay, I'm going to put the bags in the car." He ruffled Jasmine's hair as he went past. "Don't worry, Jasmine. We'll be on the beach this afternoon!"

Max was still lying huddled under the hedges, his leg throbbing with pain. He felt weak and dizzy, and he couldn't stand up. He was so scared. What was going to happen to him? Molly had no idea where he was—he didn't even know where he was.

He still wasn't really sure what had happened, either. He'd been wearily wandering along the road, then those enormous lights had swept over him, and something hit him. Then he didn't remember any more.

He wanted Molly. With a sad little snuffling noise, he laid his head down on his front paws. He couldn't move—he'd tried and his leg wasn't working. All he could do was wait, and hope. Maybe Molly would come looking for him. She wouldn't give up on him, would she?

Chapter Four
Help at Last

Jasmine bounced excitedly around the vacation cottage, racing in and out of all the rooms, and getting under Mom and Dad's feet.

"Can we go out and have a look around? Can we go and see the ocean?" she kept asking.

"After we've unloaded the car, I promise," her mom said, as she unpacked all the food they'd brought and stored it in the cupboards.

Jasmine sighed, and perched herself on the windowsill to stare out. The little cottage was right on the cliff, with only a tiny patch of grass separating it from a huge drop to the ocean. Mom and Dad had already made her promise to stay away from the edge. She had a beautiful view from there. The sun was sparkling on the water, and a couple of small boats were creeping past. The cottage was outside a town called Springfield. If they walked one way they'd get to the town, which had interesting-looking shops, and if they went the other way, they'd reach one of the many little paths down to the beach. Jasmine had been thinking that they should go and investigate the shops first, and maybe buy an ice-cream cone, but the shining water was calling to her, and now she definitely wanted to find the path down the cliff.

At last her parents had finished the unpacking and they were ready to go and explore.

"Shall we go and get an ice-cream cone?" her dad suggested. "I'd love something cool after lugging all those bags around."

"Oh, please can we go and look at the beach first?" Jasmine begged. "And can we go for a boat ride? The ocean looks so pretty out the window, really blue, with little waves. Pleeeaase!"

"I don't believe it. You're turning down ice cream?" Jasmine's mom said, laughing.

Jasmine looked thoughtful. "Well, I'm not saying I don't *want* one…."

Her dad grinned. "I'm sure we can do both. Let's take a quick look at the ocean, and then head into town."

Eagerly they set off along the road. It had a real vacation feel, not like the streets Jasmine was used to at home. This road had steep banks, and hedges full of wild flowers, and every so often something scuttled into the undergrowth as they passed. Just a little ways down from the cottage, a small white-painted sign pointing the other way said *Springfield 2 miles*. Jasmine walked ahead, looking excitedly for a path down to the ocean. "Oh, look! Here it is!" she called back, waving to her parents to catch up.

Suddenly, there was a strange little scuffling noise in the grass on the bank, and Jasmine jumped back. "Ugh! I hope it isn't a rat!" she said nervously to herself. But the scuffling was followed by a tiny whimpering sound. That definitely wasn't a rat. It sounded more like a dog....

Max had heard Jasmine calling, and for one hopeful moment he had thought it was Molly. He realized it wasn't her; this girl didn't smell right, but maybe she would help him anyway. He struggled to get up, but he couldn't. His leg hurt so much, so he just called out to her. *Please! Help me!* he whimpered.

Jasmine crouched down cautiously to peer into the grass, and saw Max's black eyes staring back at her, glazed and dull with pain. He thumped his tail wearily to show he was glad to see her.

"Oh, wow, aren't you beautiful! What are you doing here, puppy? Are you lost?" Then Jasmine saw his leg and gasped. She jumped up. "Mom! Dad! Come here, quick!"

Her parents had been strolling along, enjoying the early summer sunshine. Jasmine's anxious voice jerked them out of their daydream.

"What is it?" her dad asked, rushing up to her.

"It's a dog, a puppy, I mean. He's hurt! Oh, Dad, look at his leg...." Jasmine's voice faltered. Max's leg was badly cut and had bled a lot all over his white fur. "What are we going to do?"

"He must have been hit by a car," said Dad. "Poor little thing." He turned to

77

Jasmine's mom, who'd come running after them. "Did you see a vet in Springfield as we drove through?"

Jasmine's mom shook her head. "I'm not sure, but I think there would be. Is the little dog hurt?" she asked worriedly.

"Hit by a car, I think. We can't leave him here." He looked down at Max. "I wonder when it happened. He looks pretty weak."

Jasmine's mom nodded. "You and Jasmine stay here, and I'll go get the car, and some towels or something to wrap him in. Then we can drive him into Springfield and ask someone about a vet."

"Please hurry, Mom!" Jasmine gulped. The puppy looked so weak and

78

sick lying in the grass. "Do you think it would be okay to pick him up?" she asked. "He looks so sad."

Dad shook his head. "I don't think we should move him more than we have to. His leg might be broken, or he might have other injuries we don't know about. And if he's really hurting, he might bite you, Jasmine."

Jasmine shook her head. "I'm sure he wouldn't. He looks such a nice little dog."

Max whined again, and stretched his neck to get closer to Jasmine. She wasn't his Molly, but he could tell she was kind and friendly.

Very gently, trying not to frighten him, Jasmine put her hand out for Max to sniff.

Max licked her hand a little, then exhausted by even such a tiny effort, he slumped back.

"Oh, no. I wish Mom would hurry with the car." Jasmine looked around anxiously, then spotted their car coming along the road.

"How's he doing?" her mom asked as she jumped out, grabbing a pile of towels.

Jasmine's eyes were full of tears as she answered. "He's getting weaker. We have to hurry."

The vet's receptionist looked up as they barged through the door. "Oh, I'm sorry, we're actually just about to close—" Then she saw the puppy huddled in a towel in Jasmine's arms, and the blood seeping through the pale pink fabric. "Bring him in! This way. Mike, we've got an emergency," she called as she held open a door for Jasmine and her parents.

A tall, young man in a white jacket was looking at a computer screen inside the room, which was very clean and shiny, and smelled of disinfectant. He swung around quickly, his eyes going to the towel-wrapped bundle.

Jasmine just held Max out to him, not saying anything. She didn't know what to say, and the relief of finally getting to the vet, where someone might be able to help the poor little dog, was making her feel choked with tears.

The vet took Max and laid him carefully on the table. Max's eyes were closed, and he wasn't moving. Jasmine knew he was still alive, because she'd been watching him breathing, but even that seemed to have gotten weaker in the last few minutes.

The vet started gently checking Max over. "What happened?" he asked, without looking up.

"We don't know," Jasmine whispered. "We found him."

"We're here on vacation," her dad explained. "We were out for a walk, and Jasmine heard him crying. We guessed he'd been hit by a car."

The vet nodded. "He's very lucky. If he'd been out there much longer I don't think he would have made it. As it is," he looked up at Jasmine, "I can't promise that he will, but he's got a chance. His leg isn't broken, just badly cut, but he's lost a lot of blood, and he's very weak. I'm going to sedate him and put him on a drip, then stitch up the cut. If he turns the corner in the next couple of hours, he should be okay. But he's young, and that amount of blood loss in such a small dog…." He trailed off, but they all knew what he meant.

Jasmine gulped. "Can we wait while you do it? That would be okay, wouldn't it?" she asked her parents.

The vet smiled sympathetically at her. "Of course. You can stay in the waiting room." He was already gently gathering Max up to take him to the operating room. The puppy looked so small and helpless, and Jasmine just couldn't hold back the tears that were starting to trickle down the side of her nose.

Her mom hugged her gently, and led her out to the waiting room—and that was all they could do, just wait.

When the vet came back out into the reception area he was looking cautiously pleased. Jasmine had been leaning against her mom's shoulder, feeling worn out from her excitement and panic at finding the hurt puppy. But she jumped up immediately. "Is he going to be okay?"

The vet nodded slowly. "I think so. He's certainly got a good chance. The cut on his leg should heal well now that it's stitched, and except from that he's just bruised. Definitely no fractures. He really was lucky. He's just sleeping off the anesthetic now." He smiled down at Jasmine. "Would you like to see him?"

"Yes, please!" Jasmine nodded, and they followed the vet to a room in the back that was lined with cages. Most were empty—Jasmine guessed they didn't do that many operations on the weekend—but at one end, by the window, a small black-and-white shape was snuggled into a blue blanket. Jasmine peered in. The little puppy

was fast asleep, but he seemed to be breathing more easily, and the horrible wound on his leg was clean and neatly stitched.

"He should be fine when he wakes up," the vet said. "He'll be sleepy for the rest of the day, though. He'll have to take some painkillers in his food for a few days, and in a week or so he'll need the stitches out, but that's all. We're not open tomorrow, but I'll be here anyway at about nine if you want to stop down and see how he is."

Jasmine nodded eagerly, and then realized that her mom and dad might not want to. She gave them a pleading look.

Her dad smiled. "It's okay, Jasmine. I'd like to know how he's doing, too. Now that we've rescued him, it feels almost like he's ours."

Jasmine smiled wistfully. If only! She would love to have a dog. But she could never be lucky enough to own a beautiful puppy like this.

Chapter Five
Looking for Max

Vacation was meant to be fun, Molly thought miserably. You weren't supposed to spend all day holed up in your bedroom, because you were too sad even to ask a friend over. Molly just didn't think she could face any of her friends at the moment. Max had been missing since Friday, and now it was Monday. Molly wasn't giving up, of course, but her frantic searching was starting to seem hopeless. Listlessly, she heaved herself off her bed and went downstairs to find her mom.

Molly was pretty certain that her mom had given up hope of ever finding Max. She kept gently trying to point out to Molly that there had been no sign of him for three days, and no one had even mentioned seeing a puppy. But she was clearly still feeling guilty about letting him get out, so she agreed to go searching whenever Molly asked. They'd spent a couple of hours out looking every day so far, walking around town, asking people if they'd seen a little black-and-white puppy.

When Molly opened her mom's office door, her mom called her to the computer. "Look, I've been working on something for you," she said in a pleased voice.

Molly gulped. Max's face was staring at her from the screen, the word LOST shouting out at her. It was one of her favorite pictures of him—you could just tell he was wagging his tail like crazy, even though it was only his head showing. His tongue was hanging out a little, and his eyes gazed brightly into hers.

Her mom scrolled down to show her their phone number and a note saying when Max had disappeared, and asking people to check their garages and sheds in case Max had gotten shut in. "I thought we could print them out and put them up around town. I know we've asked most people already, but maybe the photo will jog people's memories."

Molly nodded, still feeling too choked

up to speak. It was so awful to think that she might only ever see Max again in pictures like this one. She couldn't think like that. But it was getting very hard not to….

"He looks great!" Jasmine gazed delightedly at the puppy bouncing around with an old chew-toy on Monday morning. He was so different from the weak little creature he'd been two days before. "His leg seems so much better."

The scary-looking cut was now just a neat line of stitches in a shaved patch of pinkish skin. Even the redness around the stitches was going away.

"He does look good, doesn't he? Puppies tend to heal pretty quickly," the vet agreed, smiling down at him. "He has a great character, really spunky. And he's a pedigree Old English sheepdog puppy, too, I think. Probably quite valuable."

Jasmine's mom was looking thoughtful. "If he's a pedigree puppy," she said, "it's not likely he was abandoned. He must have gotten lost. His owners must be really upset."

Mike nodded. "Yes, to be honest, I'm surprised we haven't heard anything. Springfield isn't that big. I would have thought that if anyone had lost a special dog like this, they'd have told the police, and it would have been passed on to us, too. He's too young

to have been chipped, unfortunately."
Seeing Jasmine's blank look, he
explained, "Microchipped. A lot of
dog owners have a tiny I.D. chip
injected into their dog's neck, just in
case something like this happens. It's
a really good idea."

"So you haven't heard anything?"
Jasmine said slowly, petting the little
dog's ears. She supposed she should
hope that his owners would find him,
and he'd soon be back at home and
safe, but she just couldn't. She'd been
visiting the vet every day to see how he
was—she was more interested in the
puppy than in her vacation!

"No, no one's been in touch. There
are a couple of other vets in the area,
and I've called them, and we're going

to put his picture up on our website. I think we're going to have to give him a name—I can't keep on just calling him 'puppy'!"

Jasmine smiled. "I think you should call him Lucky," she said, glad to be distracted from thinking about the puppy's real owners. "You said when we brought him in that he was lucky that the car just barely hit him, and that we found him just in time."

The vet nodded. "Mmm, that's a good idea."

The puppy looked up hopefully. He could tell they were talking about him. He liked this nice girl. She'd picked him up and carried him when he was hurt, and she kept coming to see him and play with him.

"Would you like to be called Lucky?" she said, kneeling down next to him. "Lucky? Is that a good name?"

The puppy managed a little jump up to lick her face, and barked gently, to show her he was grateful for all her petting.

"Hey, he likes it!" Jasmine said delightedly.

And so Max became Lucky....

Jasmine was quiet in the car that afternoon. They were on their way to visit some caves with underground waterfalls that her dad had found a brochure about, but she couldn't seem to feel excited about it.

"Are you all right, Jasmine?" her mom asked. "The caves should be fun, you know. Lots of interesting stuff to see."

"I know," Jasmine said, forcing a smile.

It didn't work. "You're upset about the puppy, aren't you?" her mom said gently. "But Jasmine, you must have known the vet would try to find his owners. They'll be desperate to find him, and I'm sure he misses them, too."

"I suppose," Jasmine muttered. Actually, she couldn't help feeling that whoever had lost Lucky didn't deserve to have him, letting him run off and get hurt.

"It might even be another girl like you, Jasmine," her dad put in. "Imagine if Lucky was yours, and you'd lost him.

Think how upset you'd be."

"I wouldn't have lost him!" Jasmine burst out. "Sorry," she sniffed through her tears. "I know we can't have him, but he's so sweet, and I've always wanted a dog, and just finding him like that, it seemed so perfect…."

"And you'd been dreaming of keeping him," her mom sighed. "Oh, Jasmine, I know. He is beautiful. But he really does belong to someone else. And besides, a dog … it would be such a lot of work…." But she looked thoughtfully at Jasmine's dad as she said it.

Jasmine blew her nose firmly. "Sorry. I'm all right now. Can we go to the caves? Will there be diamonds, or anything?" she said, trying hard to sound enthusiastic. It didn't really work, but Jasmine's dad gave her mom another thoughtful look.

"Molly! Hey, Molly, wait!"

Molly and her mom turned around to see Amy running toward her, followed by Amy's older sister, Sarah. "Are you going out looking for Max again? Mom says Sarah and I can come and help, if you want."

"If that's okay," Sarah added to Molly's mom.

Molly managed a small smile. It was really sweet of Amy to want to help. "We're putting up these posters," she explained, holding one out.

Amy looked at the picture. "Oh, he looks so cute," she said sadly. "Posters are a really good idea. Are you going to put them up in the grocery store? My grandma did that when her cat was missing, and someone called her the next day to say they'd seen him."

"I hadn't thought of putting them in stores, Amy," Molly's mom said. "That's very helpful. I would think most of the store owners in town would let us."

Molly nodded hopefully. "Yes, then anyone coming in from the vacation cottages along the cliffs to do their shopping would see them."

They each took a roll of tape and walked quickly along the street, taping the posters to lampposts and fences. Molly kept having to stare into Max's beautiful big eyes as she stuck his picture up all over town. It was so hard.

Amy put an arm around Molly's shoulders. "Hey," she said. "You never know. In a couple of days we'll probably be coming around and taking them all down because we've found him." She smiled at Molly, who wished she could feel so positive.

It was probably just natural puppy healing power that made Lucky's leg get better so quickly, but Jasmine liked to think that his new name had something to do with it. That and all the cuddles, games of hide-the-squeaky-bone, and snoozing on her lap that he'd been having. How could he not get well when everyone loved him so much?

"He really is doing so well," Mike said, shaking his head in amazement as he watched Lucky skidding across the floor after a new toy that Jasmine had brought with her on Wednesday morning, a fluffy knotted rope that had cost a considerable amount of her vacation spending money. "He'll be ready to go soon," Mike added thoughtfully. "I wouldn't have kept him for so long, except that I was hoping his owner might show up to claim him. No one's called about the photo on our website, though."

Jasmine gulped. "Go?" She faltered. "Um, go where?" Without really thinking about it, she snuggled Lucky close into her arms, and he licked her nose happily.

"To the rescue shelter. It doesn't look like we're going to have any luck finding his real owner, so Lucky is going to have to find someone new. I'd love to keep him here, but we're so busy. He needs more space and someone to take care of him properly."

A rescue shelter! It sounded awful. Jasmine knew that shelters did a wonderful job of taking care of strays and unwanted pets, but she still couldn't help thinking of them as grim, scary places. She didn't want Lucky to have to go to one of those!

"It's been great having you here to help take care of him," Mike said gratefully. "I don't know what we would have done without you." He grinned. "I'll tell you what. Friday is your last day here, isn't it?"

Jasmine nodded sadly. She didn't want to think about it. She was going to miss seeing Lucky so much!

"Well, to say thank you, how would you like to take Lucky out for his first walk? I'll bet his leg will be strong enough by then. You can take him for a walk on the beach. I gave him his puppy booster shots when you first brought him in, so he'd have less chance of picking up anything nasty from any other dogs here. He'll be fine to take out now. We can lend you a leash for him."

"Oh, I'd love to!" Jasmine hugged Lucky tightly, and looked at her mom, her eyes shining with excitement. She imagined them wandering along the beach together, Lucky nosing into all the good-smelling holes between the rocks, as she held on to his leash.

It would be just like having her own dog....

Chapter Six
Together Again

"Look, Lucky! The ocean!" Jasmine crouched down and pointed out over what seemed like miles of perfect sand to the water glinting blue in the sun. "I guess you've *probably* seen it before," she said doubtfully. "Anyway, Mom says that because the tide is out, we can walk along the shore to the next town. And there's a shop there that makes delicious milkshakes. Don't worry," she added, stroking his ears, "I'll carry you if you get tired."

Lucky wasn't really listening. He was taking deep, excited sniffs of the salty ocean air. It had an unmistakeable smell. And the last time he'd smelled it had been the day he lost Molly. Maybe he was close to her again! Wagging his tail briskly, he set off down the cliff path, with Jasmine trotting behind him, and her parents sauntering after them.

It was a gorgeous day for a walk, blue sky reflected in blue ocean, and the low tide leaving the sand firm and golden, with plenty of exciting things for a small dog to investigate.

"Ugh, Lucky, no...." Jasmine gently pushed him away from the dead crab he'd found. "It'll make you sick."

Lucky looked up at her reproachfully. But it smelled wonderful!

Jasmine ran after him, laughing, but every so often a small, cold thought would surface. *This is the last time.* They were going home tomorrow, early, and when they took Lucky back to the

vet later this morning, she would have to say good-bye. Unless, of course…. Jasmine just couldn't help feeling that Mom and Dad loved Lucky, too. She saw them smiling at Lucky, who was squeaking as a wave came just a bit closer than he'd thought it would. Maybe in just a few more minutes it would be time to ask….

Molly walked slowly along the beach, a little ways behind her mom and dad. Every so often she called for Max, but there was no hope in her voice anymore. She was only doing it because if she didn't, it meant she'd given up, and that meant she was never going to see him again. At least if she was still looking, she could tell herself there was a chance.

Her dad had taken off work today so they could have a long weekend together, and he and Molly's mom tried to cheer her up by suggesting a walk along the beach to Springfield. Usually it was something she loved—it was so exciting knowing that you were

112

racing the tide, and there were so many paths up the cliff that it wasn't really dangerous. But today, all Molly could think about was doing this walk with Max.

Molly sighed miserably. Max would have loved the beach so much. She could imagine him so easily, bounding through the sand, barking at the seagulls. Just like the little dog she could see way up the beach with another family, dragging a girl her own age along as he chased the waves. A sick, miserable tide of jealousy swept over Molly as she watched them. She blinked tears back from her eyes. The dog even *looked* like Max.

Molly sniffed determinedly and

looked away. "Max! Max!" she called hoarsely. "Here, Max, come on!"

Nothing happened. Molly wiped her arm across her eyes, and continued on after her mom and dad, staring at the stones. Maybe it was time to stop searching. She was just making herself feel worse.

Up the beach, Lucky stood listening intently, his black ears perked. He leaned forward, pulling on his leash. There were people walking along the beach, and one of them looked like Molly.

Forgetting that he was on a leash, and that his leg was still a little sore,

Lucky raced down the beach, barking excitedly, and dragging Jasmine stumbling behind him.

"Jasmine! Are you all right?" her mom called, seeing her fighting to keep up. She and Jasmine's dad hurried after them.

Molly looked up when she heard the barking, and her stomach twisted miserably. The puppy sounded just like Max, too. In fact…. Molly narrowed her eyes, and stared. It looked like Max because it *was* Max, hurling himself down the beach toward her, towing that girl.

Molly started to run, overtaking her mom and dad.

Max raced toward Molly even faster, desperate in case he lost her again. In a flurry of fur and sand, he flung himself at her, barking and wagging his tail and climbing into her lap as she knelt down to hug him.

"Max! Oh, Max! You came back! Where have you been? I can't believe I found you!" Molly gasped into his fur.

116

Max gave an overjoyed woof and licked the tears off her face.

"His name's Lucky," a small voice said sadly.

Molly suddenly remembered that Max was wearing a leash, and somebody else was on the other end of it. She looked up to see a blond, curly-haired girl staring down at Max.

"Or that's what we called him, anyway," the girl said, and sniffed. "I suppose he's yours, isn't he...?"

She looked like she was trying really hard not to cry, and Molly stood up slowly, cuddling Max close. "Um, yes. He climbed out the window. Exactly a week ago. My mom left it open and he got out, and we've been looking for him ever since."

"Oh." Jasmine nodded. That explained it then. "He got hit by a car," she told Lucky's real owner. "We found him. We're here on vacation."

118

Molly gasped in horror. "Hit by a car! Is he okay?"

Jasmine showed Molly the cut on Max's leg. "He was really lucky. The car just caught his leg, but it's healing really well. I've been visiting him every day." She sniffed again, and a tear rolled down her cheek. "I'm glad you've got him back, because he looks happy being back with you ... but I really wish we'd walked along the beach the other way!" And she turned and started stumbling away, feeling as though she couldn't bear to watch that other girl cuddling Lucky, *owning* him.

"Hey!" Molly called after her, but by this time both sets of parents had come hurrying up, and Jasmine's mom was holding her tightly. Molly saw the girl hiding her face in her mom's jacket, as everyone tried all at once to explain what was going on. Jasmine's mom took her to sit on a rock away from the others, and found some tissues, and Jasmine's dad explained how they'd found Max.

"We really can't thank you enough," Molly's dad said, shaking his head. "Max could have died."

"It was just so lucky that Jasmine found him," Molly's mom said, petting Max's head gently. "I can't believe we've got him back."

Jasmine's dad smiled. "He's a great little dog. I have to tell you, we'd pretty much decided that we were going to keep him." He looked over at Jasmine. "Jasmine doesn't know that. She took care of him so well. I think we'll have to give her a while to stop missing him, but then we'll think about getting a puppy of our own."

"Oh!" Molly gasped as a great idea hit her. "Mom! Jasmine could have Max's brother!"

121

"Oh, Molly, I'm not sure," her mom said doubtfully.

"There's another boy puppy in the litter Max came from," Molly explained to Jasmine's dad. "Couldn't we take them to see him?" she begged her parents. "I bet Jasmine would love him. He really looks like Max."

Jasmine's dad looked thoughtfully over at Jasmine and her mom. "I don't know. I guess we could see." He walked toward them. "Jasmine, listen, we have an idea...."

Jasmine stood in Mrs. Hughes's large kitchen, feeling miserable, and trying not to show it. She should be really excited. Lucky (she couldn't call him Max) had found his real owners again, and wouldn't have to go to a rescue shelter. *And* her mom and dad had just told her that even though they couldn't keep Lucky, they did want to get a dog, and Lucky's brother was for sale. But Jasmine felt that it was like everyone was expecting her to adore this strange puppy right away, after she'd spent a week falling in love with Lucky.

Lucky had been left in Molly's parents' car with Molly's dad, because it might confuse him to see his brother and sisters again. The three puppies who hadn't gone to new homes yet were playing with a squishy ball, jumping all over their mom and dad, who were huge! Jasmine could see why Molly had thought of her plan—one of the puppies did look almost exactly like Lucky.

"So, what do you think, Jasmine?" her mom asked anxiously.

"Um...." Jasmine didn't know what to say. It was awful. Molly and her parents were trying to be kind, and she felt really guilty. Trying to hide how she felt, Jasmine knelt down to play with the puppies, although she didn't want to. They looked at her inquisitively, their bright eyes questioning, their ears pricking up. Jasmine couldn't help smiling a little. They were so sweet.

The boy puppy with Lucky's same pirate eye patch gave a bark. It was so clearly an invitation, or possibly even an order—*play with me!*

Jasmine giggled at the bossy little dog, and rolled the ball toward him. He yapped delightedly and pounced, flinging his paws out to make a grab for it before his sisters did.

Unfortunately the ball rolled away and he landed on his nose. He sat up and whined, not really that hurt, but embarrassed and a bit upset.

"Aw…." Jasmine picked him up and cuddled him.

The puppy snuggled into her arms, the ball forgotten as he enjoyed being cuddled. He nuzzled his nose under her chin lovingly, and Jasmine laughed as his cold, wet nose brushed her ear.

Then a sharp, shocking memory of Lucky doing just the same thing made Jasmine put the puppy down suddenly. Surprised, he whined, wanting more petting, his big eyes pleading. "Sorry, little one," Jasmine muttered, rubbing him behind the ears. I just…."

The puppy clambered into her lap and licked her cheek forgivingly. His tongue managed to be soft and rough at the same time, and Jasmine wriggled and laughed. He was tickling! Suddenly something inside her that had frozen up when Lucky raced away from her on the beach melted, and she gave Lucky's brother a big hug. Holding him tightly, she stood up carefully, and looked around at her parents.

"Do you think we could call him Lucky, too?"

The Homeless Puppy

Contents

For Robin and William

Chapter One
Harry All Alone

"Beth, we need to go now," her dad told her gently. They didn't have much time before they needed to leave for the airport.

Beth didn't answer. She just stroked Harry's soft white head and chestnut-brown ears. She couldn't stop the tears from rolling down her cheeks. The puppy jumped up, placing his paws on her shoulder, and licked them away. "Oh, Harry, I'm going to miss you so much. I don't want to say good-bye," she whispered.

Her voice was so sad that Harry's curly tail stopped wagging. What was Beth talking about? It didn't sound good. He hoped they could leave this place soon. It was too noisy, and it smelled odd. There seemed to be a lot of other dogs here; he could hear them barking and growling and whimpering. He wanted to go back to his nice home.

"Here's his basket, and his toys," Beth's mother said, putting them into the cage. "I'm sorry, but we really do need to go, Beth; we have to go to the airport soon. It's going to be so exciting, isn't it?"

Harry watched his basket, his favorite red rubber bone, and squeaky fish being put into the wire cage. Beth squeaked the fish for him a couple of times, then rubbed her hand across her eyes. Harry gave a puzzled whine, looking up at Beth with his big brown eyes. What was going on?

"Oh, Mom, he knows something bad is happening," Beth said, as she got to her feet.

"Don't worry," the girl from the animal rescue shelter said gently. Her name was Sally and she seemed nice, but Beth wished she'd never had to meet her. "He'll find a good home really soon, I'm sure. He's such a sweet little dog. Puppies are always easy to find homes for, and Jack Russells are a popular breed."

Beth nodded, wiping her tears away with her sleeve. She supposed she should be glad about that — she certainly didn't want Harry to be here at the shelter forever, all miserable in a little cage. But she didn't want anyone else to have him, either! He was hers.

She'd only had him for two months,

when her dad broke the news to her that his company was sending him to Britain for three years. At first it had seemed so exciting, going to live in London, but almost at once she'd thought of Harry. Would he like it there?

And then Dad had said Harry couldn't come. That it would be too difficult with quarantine, and they would be living in a city apartment that wouldn't be suitable for a dog. Harry had to stay behind, and since they had no one to leave him with, he had to go to the shelter — a home for unwanted dogs. Which didn't seem fair, because Beth did want him, very much.

"We'll write to you to let you know when Harry's settled with a new owner," Sally promised. "Really soon. I know he's going to find a wonderful home."

Beth wanted to shout out that he had a wonderful home, but she nodded, and her dad led her out, which was good, because she was crying so much she couldn't see.

Harry whimpered, calling after her and scratching at the wire door. Beth was crying! There was something wrong, and she was going away from him. He howled for two hours, and then he was so exhausted he fell asleep.

When he woke up, she still hadn't come back.

"Oh, just look at this one," Grace said longingly. "A Labrador. Isn't she beautiful?"

Mom smiled at her. "We don't have the room, Grace, you know that. Even though she is beautiful. Such pretty eyes."

"Maybe a small dog, like a Jack Russell, then!" Grace started frantically scanning through the shelter website to see if they had any smaller dogs. "They're those cute little terrier dogs that used to hunt rats. They're really clever. And small! We've got room for one of those, definitely." Grace looked hopeful.

"No, we don't. And you'll need to get off the computer soon, Gracie, because I have to get on to the real estate website again, and see if any more apartments have come up." The Winters were looking to move at the moment, because there just wasn't enough room for them all in their current apartment, especially now that Grace and her brother, Danny, were getting older.

"It's no use, Gracie." Danny sighed, as he squeezed behind the computer chair to make some more toast. The computer was squashed into one corner of the kitchen. "I've been trying to convince Mom and Dad to get a dog for years."

Mom frowned at him. "Don't you start, Danny. You both know we just don't have the space. It's not fair to shut a dog up in an apartment, even a little dog. And definitely not on the seventh floor!"

Grace nodded. She knew it really, but every so often she managed to convince herself it wasn't true, just for a minute.

She went back to stirring her cereal, imagining running through the park with a beautiful black Labrador or a bouncy little brown-and-white Jack Russell scampering beside her. If they were moving anyway.... Was it too much to hope for a house with a yard? She licked her spoon dreamily.

"Don't get food on the keyboard, Grace!" Mom warned.

"Hey!" Danny had paused behind Grace's chair with his plate of toast, and was leaning over her shoulder. "Gracie, look! Mom, come and see!"

"I'm never going to get on my computer," Mom muttered, coming over to look at the screen. "Fairview Animal Rescue Shelter. You're still on the dogs' home website? Danny, haven't we all just agreed we can't have a dog?"

"Yes, but look. Our Fantastic Volunteers! People who help at the shelter." He grabbed the mouse and clicked on the link. "Look, they get to walk the dogs!" Danny beamed at Grace. "We could do that, couldn't we? I know we can't have our own dog, but we could borrow some. It would be like having lots of dogs!"

Grace practically pushed her nose up against the screen. There was a big photo of a hopeful-looking dog, with a leash in its mouth. Bonnie was her name, apparently. "Could we do it, Mom?" she asked eagerly. "The shelter's not far from here. Only a couple of streets away, on the other side of Fairview Park."

142

"Sounds like a good idea to me." Dad had walked in, and was staring at the computer now, too. "Anything that gets you out in the fresh air and not watching TV is good news. Does it say when they're open? I'll take you over there later, if you'd like."

Danny scanned the page. "We're always looking for more volunteers," he read. "Please drop by the shelter!"

Grace smiled up at Dad delightedly. "You really mean it?" she breathed. She hadn't really expected to be allowed a dog, and this was much, much better than nothing!

Harry was lying in his basket, with his nose shoved firmly into his blue cushion. It smelled like Beth's house — his house — and it shut out the smells of other dogs. He couldn't understand why Beth had left him here, and why she hadn't come back. Beth had brushed him and fed him

144

and loved him. She had run into the house to find him and play with him as soon as she got home from school. What had gone wrong? He hadn't been naughty, he was sure.

He could still hear the other dogs barking and whining, no matter how hard he tried to bury his head in the cushion. But then he heard the sound of footsteps. Slowly, he crept out of his basket, and went to peer through the wire door of the cage. Maybe Beth was coming back. She might even be waiting for him out there! He sprang up against the wire hopefully, and from further up the corridor Sally turned around to look at him.

145

"Hey, Harry...," she said very gently. "You decided to come and see what's going on, did you?"

Harry's ears went back, and his tail sagged again. Beth wasn't there. Just that woman, Sally, who smelled like other dogs. He slunk back to his basket, and Sally sighed. She hoped Harry wasn't going to have a really hard time.

Harry thought miserably about home. It felt like now was the time he'd normally be curling up at the end of Beth's bed. His basket was usually only for daytime naps; he always slept with Beth. She'd probably have given him one of his favorite bone biscuits, too. He sighed, and snuffled sadly. She would come back, wouldn't she?

Chapter Two
A New Friend

Grace and Danny went to school around the corner from each other, Grace at the elementary school and Danny at the high school. So Danny usually walked Grace home, except on Tuesdays when Grace had ballet. But today, Mom was meeting them so they could all go to the animal rescue shelter, and sign up to be volunteers.

They'd gone on Saturday, but it had been really busy, and the staff had asked them to come back during the week so they could meet the dogs when everything was less hectic.

"Oh, where is she?" Grace swung her school bag impatiently.

"She's not even late yet! We were finished early for once," laughed Danny. "Hey, which dog do you want to take out? I really liked that big Golden Retriever on the website. He was great — I bet he runs like the wind!"

Grace smiled. "I don't care. Any of them. Oh, look, there's Mom!" Grace ran over to her. "You took forever! Can we go right there?"

Mom laughed. "Yes, but I just want to stop at the supermarket for a few things, okay?" She winked at Danny.

"Mo-om!" Grace's expression was tragic.

"She's kidding, Gracie!" said Danny. "Honestly, you're so gullible. Come on, let's get going."

Grace, Danny, and Mom stood in the rescue shelter reception area waiting for Sally, the manager, who was going to show them around. There was a constant noise of dogs barking and howling.

"You get used to it after a while," Mandy the receptionist said, smiling. "Think how happy you'll be making them, taking them out for walks. And it's not only walking. With some of the dogs it's just about companionship, a little playing or petting. I'm afraid some of them have been badly treated, and we need to help them to trust people again."

"But none of them is dangerous?" Mom asked anxiously. "I wouldn't like Danny or Grace to be with any dogs that might bite."

"No, no." The receptionist shook her head. "Volunteers only take out dogs that we trust completely." She grinned at them. "The only thing you need to worry about is not getting too attached! I've got three dogs from here, the ones I simply couldn't resist! You just have to remember that all the dogs are going to be adopted eventually, or we hope so anyway. So don't let yourselves get too fond of them, okay?"

Grace peeked through the glass door, looking at the dogs peering back at her from their cages. How could she not fall in love with them all?

"Grace, did you hear?" Mom said gently. "Don't get too attached!"

Grace turned back and nodded. She would try....

The rescue shelter wasn't too busy, so Sally took Grace and Danny and Mom around to meet some of the dogs they'd be able to walk. There were so many — Grace was torn between being glad there were lots of dogs for her to get to know, and sad that they all had no homes of their own. It was heartbreaking when the dogs jumped up at the doors of their cages, their tails wagging desperately, licking her fingers, clearly begging for her to love them and take them home.

"Oh, this one's beautiful." Grace knelt down in front of one of the wire-fronted

cages to look at a little brown-and-white Jack Russell. "He's only a puppy!"

Harry looked up hopefully. Grace's voice sounded a little bit like Beth's. But his ears flopped back again when he saw her — just another girl. He turned around in his basket so he didn't have to look at her.

Grace gave him a surprised look. All the other dogs had been desperate for attention, and had wanted all the petting and cuddling they could get. But this little puppy seemed to want them to go away!

"This is Harry," Sally explained. "He's our newest arrival. He was left with us a week ago by a family who were moving to Britain quite suddenly. The girl he belonged to was about your age, Grace. She was really sad to leave him."

"Oh, wow," Grace muttered. She couldn't imagine. Harry looked really young. The other girl couldn't have had him for all that long before she had to give him away.

"He looks pretty miserable," Danny

154

said, crouching down to get a good look at Harry in his basket.

Sally nodded. "Yes, he's really missing Beth, his old owner. He is eating, but not much, and he won't respond to any of us when we try to cheer him up. I think he's still hoping that Beth's coming back for him."

"That's so sad," Grace said, her voice wobbling. "I wish there was something we could do to help."

Sally looked at her thoughtfully. "Harry isn't ready to go out for walks yet, Grace. If you wanted to spend time with him, it would have to be here at the shelter. Probably just sitting with him in his cage, letting him get used to trusting another person. It's sad, but we just don't have the time for that very often, with so many dogs to take care of."

Grace looked up at Sally, her eyes shining. "But I would love that!" she said gratefully. "Mom, is it okay? Do you mind if I stay here while you and Danny walk your dogs?"

"Well, as long as it's all right with Sally...," Mom said doubtfully.

"Honestly, you'd be doing us a favor," Sally assured them. "We're short-staffed, and we've all been feeling really bad that no one's had time to work with Harry yet. But Grace, don't expect too much to happen at first, okay? It might be a long, slow job. Poor Harry's really moping."

Grace nodded, looking at Harry's smooth little back, as he lay curled into a ball in his basket. His nose was

156

tucked under his paws, as though he was trying to shut out the world. She would take it really slow.

"I'll let you into the cage, then just sit down quietly to start with, not too close to him," Sally told her. "Then I'm afraid it's just all about waiting. See what he does. But if you spend some time with him every time you come, hopefully it will help him. I'll be close to make sure you're both doing okay." She opened the door for Grace, and Grace slipped inside, trying to be as quiet as she could.

Harry raised his head suspiciously and glared at her. It was that girl again. What was she doing in his cage? He huffed angrily through his nostrils, and

Grace tried not to giggle. It was such a funny little noise. She leaned against the wall of the cage and watched Harry, as he turned himself away and snuggled sadly into his basket again. It wasn't quite what she'd imagined, sitting on the floor just looking at a dog, instead of racing around the park. But Harry was so little, and his face when he first looked up at her had been so hopeful, and then so terribly sad.

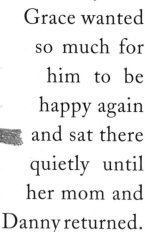

Grace wanted so much for him to be happy again and sat there quietly until her mom and Danny returned.

158

Harry had always been a friendly dog when he lived with Beth, but he liked his own space, too. He didn't really enjoy being cooped up with a lot of other dogs. And he hated being shut up in a cage. No matter how hard the staff tried to exercise all the dogs, they had to stay in their cages for a lot of the day. As for the noise — Harry was a sensitive little dog, and the sound of barking made him want to hide under his cushion.

What made it worse was that other people kept bothering him. He was taken out of the cage and given to them to hold. He wished they would just leave him alone so he could wait for Beth to come back and get him.

When was she coming back? He was still hoping that she would, but he was getting less sure every day.

That first day, Harry hadn't even looked at Grace. She wanted to go to the rescue shelter on Tuesday, but she had ballet class. But on Wednesday, when Grace visited, Harry actually stood up in his basket and leaned over to give her a considering sniff. Hmm. So it was her again.

On Friday she was back, so he licked her fingers, just to be polite. When she left, he watched her walking down the hallway. She smelled nice, and he wondered if she would come again. On Saturday, he sat up in his basket when she opened the cage, and when she crouched down next to him, he put his paws on her knee, encouraging her to pet him.

"Oh, Harry...." Grace breathed delightedly. He was happy to see her!

Harry hadn't been planning to make friends with the girl, but she was quiet and gentle, and she reminded him of Beth. It was nice to be petted again, and told what a handsome boy he was. He was still waiting for Beth to come back, of course, but there was no harm in letting this nice girl — Grace, the others called her — make a big deal over him.

The next Monday, Sally walked past Harry's cage to see him curled up in Grace's lap while she stroked his ears. Grace was staring down at him with a little smile on her face. She was imagining that Harry was hers, and that they weren't at the rescue shelter; they were sitting on the grass in her yard, a nice big yard, just right for a dog to play in. None of the apartments that they'd seen in their house-hunting had had yards, but this was only a dream, after all....

"You've done really well with him," Sally said, smiling.

Grace jumped slightly — she hadn't noticed Sally coming. Harry grumbled a little when she moved, and turned himself around to get comfy again.

Sally watched him, looking pleased. "You've got a great feeling for animals, Grace. You've been so patient, and it's really paid off with Harry. We'll start trying to introduce him to more visitors now, I think. We'd really like to find a new home for him soon."

Grace only nodded. She couldn't trust herself to say anything. She didn't want Harry to be adopted yet — then she'd never see him again.

Grace frowned at the knitting pattern. She was trying to make a little teddy bear for Harry to have in his basket, but knitting was a lot trickier than it looked when her grandmother did it. She sighed. She had a feeling that it wasn't going to look like the picture, but then Harry would probably chew it to pieces anyway. She just really wanted him to have something to remember her by. Visitors at the shelter kept saying how cute he was, and she was sure he was going to be adopted soon. Grace sniffed, and a tear smudged the crumpled pattern.

"Grace," Danny called around the door. "We've got to go and look at this apartment with Mom and Dad."

Grace frowned. Her room at the

moment was more like a cupboard, but she liked it, even if there wasn't enough space for a desk and she had to do her homework on her bed. It was comfy like that, anyway.

The new apartment was really nice, with a much bigger room for Grace. She could imagine all her dog posters up at last, with all that space, and lots of shelves for her tiny china animals and her books. But it was a second-floor apartment — with no yard.

"So, what did you think?" Dad asked, as they were walking back home. "I really liked it."

Mom nodded. "Me, too. Beautiful kitchen. And your room was great, wasn't it, Grace?"

Grace shrugged.

"What is it?" Dad asked. "Didn't you like it?"

"I'd much rather have a tiny

bedroom, and a yard, so that we could have a dog. I really would. I don't need a big room, honestly."

"She's right," Danny put in. "A yard would be terrific."

Mom sighed. "I know how much you two want a dog, and I've been really impressed with the way you've worked so hard at the rescue shelter. But I still wouldn't feel happy about leaving a dog alone all day. We'll have to think about it."

But she gave Dad a thoughtful look, and leafed through the list of apartments that the real estate agent had given them. Maybe they could find something....

Chapter Three
An Outside Adventure

Harry had started to look forward to Grace's visits. She usually came after school, so at about half-past three he would find himself standing by the door of his cage, sometimes with his paws up on the wire, watching for her. That Friday afternoon, almost two weeks after he'd first met Grace, Harry woke up from a nice snooze in his basket, and stretched out his paws. Now, why had he woken up? Was it time to eat? No…. Ah. It was Grace time. She should be coming to play with him soon.

"Oh, he's adorable! What a beautiful little dog!"

A voice floated over to him, but it didn't sound like Grace. Harry blinked, still a little sleepy, and peered across the cage. A young woman was looking at him, and Sally was with her.

Sally opened the cage to let the woman hold Harry. He allowed her to pick him up, but he kept peering over her shoulder, looking for Grace.

"He's been with us a couple of weeks now. He's a great puppy, but he's been missing his old owner. She had to go overseas. He's cheering up a little now, but any new owners would have to take it slowly with him. Really take the time to build a relationship. And you know that Jack Russells are very energetic? They really need a lot of exercise."

The woman nodded. "I'll definitely go home and talk it over with my husband. I'll let you know very soon."

She waved good-bye to Harry as she walked down the hallway back to the reception area, and Harry wagged his tail delightedly and woofed. The woman smiled, thinking this was all for her — she didn't realize that Grace was just walking through the door behind her. She went home thinking what a sweet, affectionate little dog Harry was. He'd obviously taken to her.

Grace gave the woman a worried look as the door swung shut. Not another person admiring Harry! Everyone who came to the rescue shelter seemed to think he was really cute. Grace had a horrible feeling that Harry would be going to a new home soon.

"Hey, Grace! I'm making some coffee; do you want some juice? And there's a package of chocolate cookies. Would you like one?" Sally waved the package at Grace as she walked past the kitchen on the way to see Harry the next day. On Saturdays Grace usually played with Harry, and then tried to spend some time with any other dogs that the staff thought needed some extra attention. Sally had asked her to help with a couple of other dogs who were quite shy and needed someone patient.

"Chocolate cookies! Yes, please!"

Grace leaned against the kitchen door, nibbling her cookie. She couldn't take it with her, because the dogs would all want to share it, and chocolate wasn't good for dogs.

"You're doing really well with Harry, you know, Grace. It's made a big difference to him, your being here." Sally stirred her coffee thoughtfully. "You're going to miss him when he goes to a new home, aren't you?"

Grace nodded, her mouth full of cookie. "Mmmf."

"Now that he's so much friendlier, I don't think it's going to be all that long before he goes. He's such a sweetie. Just keep it at the back of your mind, okay? I don't want you to be upset, that's all."

Grace stared into her orange juice.

"I know...," she said at last. "I won't be upset. Really." She told herself that it was true, that she'd always known Harry would be adopted. But

173

deep down, she knew that she'd been secretly pretending that he was hers.

"Anyway, I think you could take him for a real walk today, if you'd like to." Sally grinned as Grace nearly hugged her. "Watch it with the juice! I think he's ready. Danny's here, isn't he? Your mom's okay for you to go out if he's with you, isn't she?"

"Yes." Grace nodded excitedly. "I'll tell him."

Sally smiled. "It's okay; I'll find him. You go and put Harry's leash on. He'll be so excited. He just hasn't been getting enough exercise. Jack Russells really like a couple of hour-long walks every day."

Sally was almost right. As soon as Harry saw his leash, he started jumping up wildly, leaping around and practically bouncing off the walls. He could jump easily as high as Grace's waist. She had to pin him under one arm to keep him still enough to put the leash on. "Calm down, calm down, silly boy," she whispered lovingly as he leaped up to try to lick her face.

Eventually she led him proudly out through the reception area, where Danny was waiting with Bella, the Labrador they'd first seen on the rescue shelter website.

It felt so exciting, walking out of the shelter with Harry on his leash — it was a blue one that had been his when he belonged to Beth's family, and he looked wonderful.

"Remember how I showed you the way to keep him under control!" Sally called after them.

Grace looked down at Harry and grinned. Heel was a good idea, but.... He was just so excited. She had to keep gently pulling him back every time he lunged after a strange smell, or wanted to chase a fluttering leaf.

Harry was blissfully happy. He hadn't been outside the shelter in so long — but as soon as he'd seen his leash, and heard Grace say walk, he knew exactly what it meant. He loved walks. He wanted to see everything! Every bee was a possible enemy that needed chasing, every leaf had to be checked out.

Grace was glad that Sally had reminded her to keep a really good hold on Harry when they passed other dogs. A huge German Shepherd was walking along the road toward them, and Harry spotted him even before Grace did. He barked mightily (just to show the German Shepherd he wasn't scared, even if he was a little...) and tried his best to show that he was the bravest, toughest dog in the world.

The German Shepherd's owner smiled at Grace. "You've got a real little character there!"

Grace nodded breathlessly. All her energy was focused on keeping Harry under control. She hoped he wouldn't be like this with every dog in the park!

Luckily, he started to calm down after that, and by the time they were passing the shops, he was walking quite nicely.

"Hey, Grace, if I just tie Bella's leash on this hook, is it okay if I run in and see if they've got the new skateboarding magazine?" Danny asked.

Grace looked doubtfully at Harry. He didn't look like he wanted to stop. "If you're really quick!" she agreed.

"Great. Back in a minute." And

Danny disappeared inside the store. Bella sat down patiently and didn't seem to mind waiting, so Grace bent down to pet Harry.

"Hi, Grace!" Someone was calling. Grace looked around to see her friend Maya from ballet coming down the road with her sister. "I didn't know you had a dog! What's his name? Can I pet him?"

Grace blinked. "His name is Harry," she said slowly. "Yes, of course you can pet him. He's very friendly." She knew she should tell Maya that Harry wasn't actually hers, but she just didn't want to…. It was so nice to pretend that he really belonged to her. Harry was being so good, sitting and letting Maya pat him. Grace was so proud of him! And his good behavior was mostly because of all that time she'd spent with him — so why shouldn't she let Maya think that he was hers?

"Come on, Maya, we've got to go," Maya's sister told her, and Maya stood up reluctantly.

"Grace, could I come over again one day, and play with you and Harry? He's beautiful. You're so lucky!"

Maya had come over to play a couple of times before, and they'd had a great time. But what was Grace supposed to say now? If Maya came over, she'd know that Grace didn't really own Harry.

Grace looked down at the ground. "I'll have to ask my mom," she mumbled.

Luckily, Maya's sister was in a hurry. "Come on, Maya, now!" she said, heading off down the road.

"Um, see you at ballet!" Grace called, as Maya hurried off after her sister.

181

Maya was calling something back to her, but Grace pretended not to hear. She just hoped Maya didn't think she was being unfriendly. And what was she going to say to her at ballet if Maya asked again about coming over?

Maybe she should have told Maya the truth after all....

Chapter Four
A Missed Good-bye

Harry had loved his walk to the park. The only bad thing about it was returning to the shelter. He wished that Grace hadn't brought him back here. He wasn't sure where she went between her visits, but it would be so much nicer if she could take him there with her. She seemed to be sad when they said good-bye, too, so why did she have to leave him behind?

He huddled sadly in the corner of his basket and sighed, wishing that great big dog across the hall would just be quiet. He wanted to go to sleep.

Still, Harry was a lot more cheerful than he'd been before he met Grace. His eyes were brighter, and he played in his cage, instead of being curled up in his basket all day. Everyone admired him now, and Sally was always showing him off to possible owners.

By the next weekend, Grace was starting to get really worried. The other volunteers kept telling her how much people admired him, and she could see that when she was there, too.

"It's lucky that Jack Russells need so much exercise," Grace whispered to Harry, as an elderly lady regretfully went on to look for a less energetic dog. "She really liked you. She'd have taken you if Sally hadn't pointed that out. Oh, I don't believe it, Harry, look. More people!"

A family with a boy a little younger than she was and a baby girl was looking excitedly at Harry.

"I like this one, Daddy!" the boy was saying. "He's great."

The dad looked at Harry running around Grace, and smiled. "He does look nice. Do you work here?" he asked Grace.

Grace nodded. "I volunteer after

school and on the weekends."

"We're looking for a family dog," the mother added. "Do you think that" — she looked at his name card — "Harry would be a good choice?"

Grace gulped. She looked around quickly to check that none of the staff was close enough to hear, then said quietly, "Um, I'm not sure. Jack Russells aren't great with very young children. They can be a little snappy if children bother them too much...."

It was actually true, that Jack Russells could be snappy. But Harry had never shown signs of anything like that, and Grace knew she was being mean by trying to turn them off from Harry. She just couldn't bear to see him go to someone else.

"You might want a gentler dog, with your baby," she added. "Have you seen Maggie? She's a crossbreed, but she's really sweet, and so friendly and well behaved."

Luckily, the family thought Maggie

was beautiful, and when Grace left the rescue shelter, they were talking with Sally about adopting her. But Grace felt terrible all the way home.

"What's up?" Danny asked her. He'd been exercising Bella and Frisky, a retriever, in the outdoor yard. "You haven't told me anything about all the cute stuff Harry did today. Have you managed to get him to shake hands yet? You thought he'd nearly gotten it."

Grace gave a sad little shrug. "He can almost do it. Danny, one of the families who came today really liked him. I sort of turned them off from him, because they had a baby and Jack Russells aren't good with little kids, but it was mostly because I didn't want them to take him…. I don't want him to go," she explained.

"Oh, Gracie," Danny said, putting an arm around her shoulders. "Sally and Mandy warned us when we started. You promised you wouldn't fall in love with any of them."

"I know!" Grace wailed. "But Harry's so beautiful, Danny. I don't want anyone to have him except me!"

Danny sighed. "Well, you managed to turn those people off today, but Gracie, you can't be there every time someone likes him. It's going to happen, you know, sooner or later."

"Some help you are," Grace sniffled, but she knew it was true.

It was about to happen even sooner than Grace had thought. Mrs. Jameson, the young woman who'd asked Sally about Harry, came back that Sunday. She was a perfect owner. No small children, a big yard for him to play in, and she worked from home some of the time so he wouldn't be too lonely. The rescue shelter staff were delighted.

So was Harry. He'd seen Grace come in just after the lady once before, and he assumed they belonged together. So when he saw Sally loading all his toys into his basket, and bringing out his leash for this lady, he was sure that she must be taking him to see Grace. He didn't understand why Grace wasn't

190

coming to get him, but he was sure that that was where they were going.

"What do you think of your new home, Harry?" As Mrs. Jameson put his basket down in the kitchen, Harry looked around with interest. It was nice. Lots of space, and many things to sniff and explore. He wondered where Grace was. He sniffed behind all the cupboards, then checked under the table in case she was hiding. Hopefully she would come soon.

Grace hadn't been able to go to the rescue shelter for a few days. They'd been busy apartment-hunting and today was Tuesday, so she had to go to ballet after school.

She crept into the changing room. Luckily, Mom had dropped her off a little late, so Maya would probably be already changed and in the ballet studio, and Grace wouldn't have to talk to her before the class started. She just knew that Maya was going to ask about Harry, and she still hadn't figured out what to say.

Quickly, Grace changed into her leotard, and put her hair up, then she sneaked into the studio just in time. She looked around for Maya as they did their warm-up routine, but she couldn't see her. All during class, Grace watched for Maya, but she never arrived.

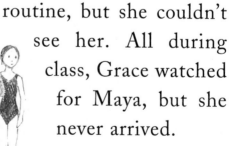

Grace had gotten away with it — for one week, anyway.

Grace ran into the rescue shelter on Wednesday afternoon, dashing ahead of Danny. She'd really missed Harry over the last few days; it felt like forever since she'd seen him. And she'd finally finished Harry's toy last night — she couldn't wait to give it to him.

She ran to Harry's cage, and gasped. He was gone! There was a friendly-looking black spaniel there instead, who woofed an excited hello and came to greet her. Grace stood by the cage, her heart racing, hardly feeling the spaniel licking her fingers.

193

Maybe he'd been moved? Yes, that was it. Harry must be in one of the other cages, that was all. She said good-bye to the spaniel, who stared after her sadly, and searched the rest of the kennel area. Every cage was full, but none of the dogs was Harry. Sally met her coming in from the outdoor area, her head hanging.

"Oh, Grace! I didn't know you were here yet." Sally looked at her worriedly. "Grace, I'm sorry. I really wanted to tell you before you saw that he was gone."

Grace nodded.

"A really nice lady took him," Sally promised. "She has a big yard for him to run in."

"Oh," Grace whispered. Then she turned and ran back down the hallway.

Danny was putting a leash on one of the other dogs, a big Greyhound that he really liked. He straightened up when Grace brushed past him. "Hey, what's the matter? Grace? Where are you going?" He stared after her, then followed. He had a horrible feeling he already knew what had happened.

Harry lay in his basket, staring sadly around the kitchen. He'd been at his new home for two days now, and his new owners both had to go to work today. He was all alone. He hadn't liked the noise and bustle of the rescue shelter, but it felt very strange for things to be so quiet.

And where was Grace? He had been sure that this was her house and he was going to live with her, but it had been a long time, and she still hadn't come. He was beginning to have a horrible feeling that the wrong person had brought him home, and he didn't know what to do about it.

At least it wasn't dark now. The

kitchen was very scary at night, and he howled for someone to come and keep him company. At Beth's house he had been allowed to sleep on her bed, never shut up on his own all night.

Mrs. Jameson had come downstairs and comforted him the first night, but she wasn't the person he really wanted. Mr. Jameson patted him occasionally, but he kept sniffing, and he sneezed whenever Harry came close to him. His sneezes were very loud, and scary. Harry was spending a lot of time locked in on his own in the kitchen, because he and Mr. Jameson didn't seem to be able to be in the same room together.

Harry sighed. Maybe someone would come and play with him soon.

Maybe even Grace. He really hoped so. But Beth had gone and not come back. Had Grace left him now, too?

Chapter Five
Feeling Lonely

Danny went to the rescue shelter on his own on Thursday. He tried to get Grace to come with him, but she wouldn't. When he got back, he went to her room and tried to cheer her up with funny stories about Finn, his current favorite at the shelter. Finn was half Labrador, half no-one-knew-what, except that he was very big and very hungry. Danny had had to admit to Sally that Finn had found half a packet of mints in his pocket and wolfed them down before Danny could stop him. But luckily, Sally had come to look at Finn, and said she thought it would probably take about six packets of mints to do anything to him; he had an iron stomach.

The story only earned Danny a very small smile. But on Friday after school, he set to work again. "You know, it's not fair on Sally and all the other dogs if you don't go," he pointed out.

"What do you mean?" Grace asked worriedly. She liked Sally a lot; she really didn't want to upset her.

"Well, she's used to having you there to help. If we don't go, the dogs won't get as many walks. I'm taking Finn out again today, but what about Bella and Jake and Harrison? I can't walk all of them, Grace, and not many other people come in to help during the week."

Grace nodded. He was right. It was just hard to imagine going back to the rescue shelter and Harry not being there.

"And don't forget how good everyone at the shelter said you were with the dogs. It'd be a real shame if you stopped going." Danny looked at her hopefully. "Should I call Mom and tell her I'm not dropping you off at home because you're coming with me?" He whipped his cell phone out of his pocket.

Grace sighed. "I suppose so."

"Great!" Danny cheered.

Sally said that Jake really needed a walk, and that Grace and Danny could take him and Finn to the park together.

Grace tried not to be too miserable — it wasn't fair on Jake for a start; he was a beautiful dog, a Westie with a soft white coat. It was difficult, though. She couldn't help remembering the wonderful walk she'd had with Harry.

Finn dragged Danny off to bark at squirrels in the trees on one side of the park, and Grace wandered slowly around the play area with Jake. He was an elderly dog, whose previous owner had died, and he liked gentle walks.

"Grace! Hi!" Someone was calling from the swings, and Grace looked over and saw Maya. Grace smiled and waved at her, but then her smile faded. How was she going to explain Jake?

"Did you miss me at ballet last week?" Maya called, slipping off the swing and running over. "I had a tummy bug, and Mom said if I was missing school, I couldn't go to ballet." Maya looked down at Jake, and then up again, confused. "That's not the same dog you had last time, is it? The other one had a pointier nose."

"Um, yes…," Grace muttered.

"Wow, do you have two dogs now?" Maya asked excitedly.

Grace stared down at Jake and shook her head. She was too embarrassed to look at Maya. "I don't have a dog. They aren't mine. Neither of them." Then she pulled on Jake's leash and suddenly dragged him off across the park.

Maya stood staring after them, looking surprised and a little upset.

Grace found Danny trying to persuade Finn to leave the squirrels alone, and told him what had happened. She was almost crying.

"So you just ran off?" Danny asked in disbelief.

"Yes...," Grace admitted.

"Why didn't you explain? I'll bet she would've understood."

"No, she wouldn't. I'd have to admit that I lied to her when I met her that time with Harry. I let her think he was mine, Danny. I never actually said it, but I didn't tell her he wasn't, either."

Danny blinked as he figured that one out. "I still think she'd understand if you explained it to her. You'll have to at some point anyway. She's bound to ask you at ballet."

"I could stop going to ballet...," Grace suggested desperately.

"Like Mom's going to let you do

that! How can you be so good at getting dogs to understand you, but too shy to talk to people?" Danny shook his head. "Nope, you'll just have to explain. Is she still here?"

They looked over at the play area. Maya was there, talking to her sister.

"Come on!" And Danny grabbed Grace's arms and marched her and Finn and Jake across the park.

Grace slowly approached Maya, looking embarrassed.

"Go on," Danny nudged her.

"I'm so sorry," Grace muttered. "I didn't mean to pretend Harry was mine, but when you thought he was, it was so nice. I really, really wanted him to belong to me."

Maya gave her a confused and slightly suspicious look. "So neither of them is yours? Who do they belong to, then?"

Grace sighed sadly. "The animal rescue shelter. Danny and I go and help there after school. We take the dogs for walks."

"Ohhh." Maya nodded.

"I didn't mean to run off. It's just that I suddenly realized you'd know I'd lied to you and I didn't know how to explain everything." Grace looked at Maya hopefully. Danny had been so sure that if she explained, Maya would be okay with it. Was he right?

"If you liked Harry so much, why didn't you take him home?" Maya asked.

"Mom says we can't fit a dog in our

apartment." Grace sighed. "But Harry was so sad when he first came to the shelter. I spent a long time trying to cheer him up, and it was almost like he was mine. When you thought he actually belonged to me, it was like my wish come true."

"At least you can see him at the shelter," Maya said. "It sounds like fun."

Grace sighed. "I can't anymore. Someone else adopted him over the weekend; that's why I have Jake today instead. Harry's gone."

"Oh, Grace! That's so sad." They were silent for a minute, then Maya looked at her shyly. "Do you still go to the rescue shelter? Could I come with you sometime? I love dogs, too; I'd really like to see them all."

"Oh, yes! Why don't you meet us

there tomorrow?" Grace smiled. "Mom said we could definitely go on Saturday morning, didn't she, Danny? And they're always wanting more help."

Grace never even noticed that someone else was there in the park. Mrs. Jameson was working from home, and had taken Harry out for a quick walk. He was enjoying the smells — the park was full of interesting garbage cans, and squirrels, and the scents of other dogs — but he wished he was with Grace. He plodded slowly around the path, watching the other dogs, and the children playing. He wondered where Grace was now.

211

And then he saw her. Grace was over on the other side of the park — with another dog. Harry stopped in his tracks, and ignored Mrs. Jameson gently pulling on his leash. Had she forgotten him already? Harry barked and barked, pulling on his leash as hard

as he could, but she was too far away to hear him. Did Grace have another dog now? He missed her so much, as much as he'd missed Beth when she went away. Why did everyone go away? Harry sat down in the middle of the path and howled broken-heartedly.

Mrs. Jameson was worried that he might be hurt somehow. She picked him up and hurried home, where he curled up in his basket and didn't want to play all evening. He even refused to eat. He felt so lonely, and he wanted Grace to come back for him so much. Why did she have another dog now? Didn't she love him anymore?

Mrs. Jameson didn't know what was wrong with Harry, and when her husband got home from work, she told him how upset Harry seemed. "I want him to be happy here, but he doesn't seem to be settling in at all," she admitted.

Mr. Jameson sighed. "I'm not sure this is working out, either...."

Mrs. Jameson nodded sadly. "I know.

We can't just keep shutting Harry in the kitchen, and your allergy's getting worse every day."

Mr. Jameson gave her a hug. "I'm sorry. I know you really wanted a dog...."

His wife smiled. "But it isn't fair on either of you. I'll call the rescue shelter tomorrow and arrange to take him back." She sniffed. "Poor little Harry...."

Chapter Six
A Surprise Meeting

Maya and her sister were waiting outside the rescue shelter for Grace when Grace and Danny and Mom arrived on Saturday afternoon. Maya was going to stay for a couple of hours, and then her sister was coming back to pick her up. Grace was delighted to have someone to show around, and Maya loved meeting all the dogs.

They were just saying hello to Jake, the Westie, when Grace heard a familiar yap from the next cage. She turned slowly to look. Could it be....

"Harry!" Grace cried, and he bounded up to the door of the gate, leaping and barking delightedly.

"Oh, it's really you! What are you doing back here?" Grace asked, petting him through the wire.

"He seems so happy to see you," said Sally, coming up behind Grace. Sally was smiling, but she didn't sound too happy, and Grace suddenly realized that if Harry was back, it meant his new owner must have been a mistake.

"Did the people not want him after all?" she asked, gazing fondly at Harry.

Sally sighed. "Harry didn't settle in very well, unfortunately. I'm sure he would have been fine over time, but the husband turned out to be allergic to dogs, too. Poor Harry. Back here again, aren't you, sweetheart?"

Grace looked at Harry lovingly. She slipped into his cage and sat down, letting him climb all over her. She was so glad to see him again. But then a horrible thought struck her. Harry hadn't settled at his new home — was that her fault? Because she'd been spending so much time with him? If he was too fond of her, he might not want to go to a new owner.

"What's the matter?" Maya asked.

"Aren't you happy he's back?"

Grace sighed. "I am happy. But Sally said he didn't settle in at his new home. What if that's because he's spending too much time with me?"

Maya looked confused, and Grace tried to explain. "He's going to be adopted again. What if I spoil another new home for him? Maybe I just shouldn't see him anymore."

Harry lay blissfully in Grace's lap, his paws folded on his stomach, eyes closed. The only thing that could make this better would be some food. He was fairly sure dinner would be here soon....

"Harry…. Harry…." Grace was whispering to him. "I have to go, sweetie. It's time for you to eat." She lifted him gently off her lap.

Harry slid off sleepily, and looked up at her, puzzled. She was going? Again? But she'd only just come back! Grace was opening the door of his cage, and he flung himself at her, howling. No! He didn't want her to go. She might not come back again!

Grace shut the door of the cage, her fingers trembling. Harry was howling so loudly that everyone in the rescue shelter was looking around, wondering what was happening.

Sally walked quickly toward them. "Don't worry, Grace. I've got some food for him; hopefully that'll help calm him down. You go. See you soon, okay? Don't worry about Harry. He's just had a hard couple of days."

Grace nodded, blinking back tears. It was really hard to leave him when he was so upset. Maya and Danny were hurrying up the hallway toward her, looking worried.

"Maya told me Harry was back. Was that him howling?" Danny asked.

Grace nodded and sniffed. Danny gave her a hug and they headed for the door. Mom was waving to them from the reception area, telling them to hurry up.

Maya had just opened the door when there was a sudden crash, and they turned back to see that Sally had dropped Harry's food bowl. It looked like he'd jumped at the door of the cage

221

as she'd opened it, and run into her. Now he was racing between the cages, barking madly, with Sally chasing after him.

Harry settled at Grace's feet, his tail wagging desperately. Other people were allowed to take him home. Why couldn't she? She was the one he wanted to go home with!

Hopefully, he held out one paw, the way she'd been teaching him. Grace's eyes were full of tears as she crouched down to take it. Harry gave a triumphant little bark. He'd done it right. There. Surely she couldn't send him back to his cage now.

Grace picked him up, and rubbed her cheek against his smooth fur. Then she handed him back to Sally, and ran.

She couldn't bear to see him like this.

Danny, Maya, and Mom found her outside the rescue shelter, leaning against the wall and crying.

"Oh, Grace…," Mom said worriedly. "I'm sure he'll be all right in a minute." Grace gave her a disbelieving look, and Mom sighed. "Well, maybe not right away, but I'm sure he will get over it."

"But it isn't fair!" Grace sobbed. "He's always having to get over things. His first owner had to leave him, and now this one's given up on him, and he just wants to be with me and I can't have him!"

Mom put an arm around her shoulders comfortingly, and Danny asked, "Mom, isn't there any way we could have him? You know how hard Grace has worked."

"I do know, and I'm really proud of you, Grace. But Harry needs a lot of space to run around. And he'd hate being shut in his cage while we're all out during the day. I'm sorry, Grace; I wish things were different, but you know we can't have a dog at the moment."

Chapter Seven
A New Family

"He's as bad as he was when he first came," Mandy said sadly, looking at the little brown-and-white ball in the basket. It was all they'd been able to see of Harry for days.

Sally called gently, "Harry! Here, boy!" but he didn't even twitch. "It's so sad. He really adored Grace, but I can understand why she doesn't think she should visit him anymore, and it's probably for the best."

"Still, there's a family coming to see him this afternoon," said Mandy. "They saw him on the website, and they think he looks perfect. If they like him, and they can give him the time to settle in...."

They stared at Harry, still curled up silently, and Sally sighed. "Well, you never know...."

Grace didn't go to the rescue shelter at all that week. She just couldn't bear it. She had made Harry's life even harder by falling in love with him. He had to find a new home, and she was stopping him.

She just had to let him go, and the sooner, the better.

She supposed she could have gone back to the shelter and kept away from Harry, but that would be so difficult. Danny didn't even try to persuade her this time. Mom had called the shelter to talk to Sally and explain. Grace had listened to what Mom was saying, and she could tell that Sally was sad, but that she agreed with Mom. It was the best thing for Harry.

Life was very boring without the rescue shelter to go to, though, Grace thought, lying on her bed listening to her favorite CD. School, more school, hanging around at home. She'd gone to Maya's to play yesterday, which was nice, but she still missed Harry, and all the other dogs, so much.

"Grace!" Mom called from the kitchen. "Time to go!"

Grace sighed, and rolled off her bed. Another apartment to go and see.

Grace smiled politely as Sheila, the lady who owned the apartment, chatted to her about whether she liked the bedroom that would be hers. She just wished Mom and Dad would stop fussing about the bathroom and get going; she was so sick of apartment-hunting. They'd already seen this apartment anyway, yesterday, when Grace and Danny were at school. Why did they need to look at everything again?

They finished at last, and Sheila led them back toward the kitchen. "I'll just show you the yard," she said over her shoulder. "I cleaned it up a bit since you saw it yesterday, but I'm afraid I'm not much of a gardener."

Grace gasped. "A yard! There's a yard?"

Sheila turned back and smiled. "Yes. Didn't your parents tell you? The yard goes with this ground-floor apartment."

Grace looked at Mom and Dad, her eyes wide with hope. "So could we...?"

Mom nodded and laughed. "Yes! I mean, it'll take a little while before we can move in, of course. But your dad and I have talked this over, and yes, we can have Harry."

Grace flung herself at her mom and

hugged her. "You planned all this. I can't believe it!"

Her mom laughed and led her over to the window. "When we saw it, we realized how perfect it would be for you and Danny. You've both worked so hard at the rescue shelter. Now you get to have your own dog."

They looked out at the yard. It was messy, full of weeds, but Grace could just imagine Harry bounding up and down, barking joyfully as she threw a ball for him to chase.

Danny stared out, too, his face split by an enormous grin, but then he frowned. "What about us all being out in the daytime? You said we couldn't leave Harry alone all day."

Dad nodded. "It's okay. I've spoken to my bosses, and they're fine with me bringing Harry into the office some of the time. And when I have meetings, your mom should be able to stop home and give him a walk during her lunch hour."

"Oh, Dad!" Grace hugged him, and then her mom again. "Thank you so much! Can we go home and call the shelter now?"

When they got back, Grace was standing hopefully holding the phone before anyone else had even gotten their coat off. She'd even found the number on the kitchen bulletin board.

"All right, all right!" Mom laughed and took the phone.

Grace waited with her fingernails digging into her palms, listening to the ringing on the other end.

"Oh, hello. Could I speak to Sally, please? Oh, it's you, Sally. This is Amanda Winter, Grace and Danny's mom. Yes, we're all fine, thank you. We've missed you, too. But actually, we've got some good news. We're moving, and we're going to have more space in our new apartment. We think we might be able to adopt Harry after all." Mom smiled excitedly at Grace, but then there was a long pause, and the smile faded. Her voice had flattened when she next spoke. "Oh. Oh, I see. Yes, well, that's good. Yes. We should have expected it. I'll tell her. Thanks. Bye."

"Someone else has taken him, haven't they?" Grace asked, her voice shaking, and Mom nodded.

"Oh, Gracie, I'm so sorry." She sighed. "Sally said he's gone to a family this time. The children aren't too young for a dog, and they're all excited to have him. He'll have a wonderful time...." But she couldn't make the words sound happy.

"If only we'd found the apartment sooner!" Grace wailed.

"It's terrible luck," Mom agreed. "We'll just have to try and be happy for Harry. I know it's hard."

Dad picked up Grace and hugged her, even though he was always saying she was too big for him to do that now. Danny sat at the kitchen table with his chin on his hands, staring out the window. "I can't believe we just missed him," he muttered. "It isn't fair...."

"You probably don't want to think about this right now," Dad said slowly. "But — there are other dogs. Lots of dogs at the shelter who need a home."

"Not yet," Grace interrupted. "We couldn't just yet."

"No, I know. But think about it. Harry's found a nice home. But we could give a good home to another dog."

Grace nodded, and sniffed. At last she said slowly, "Maybe. We could have Finn. He's your favorite, isn't he, Danny? The one who ate your mints?" Her voice was shaking.

Danny nodded. "But I think he's too big, even for an apartment with a yard. Harry would have been perfect...."

"He would, wouldn't he?" Grace tried to smile. "I suppose at least now I can go and help at the rescue shelter again, without worrying about upsetting Harry. Oh, I hope he likes the new people! He deserves a better chance this time!"

Chapter Eight
The Perfect Match

It was a little more than a week later, and Grace was sitting in her new bedroom. It was much bigger than her old one, but she hadn't finished unpacking her things yet. She just couldn't summon the energy. Mom kept telling her to get going, but Grace couldn't help stopping to look out her window, imagining Harry playing out there. If she half-closed her eyes, she could almost see him, hiding under that big bush, getting ready to leap out at her....

Grace rubbed her hand across her eyes. Harry had a new home now. It was a nice family, Sally had said, when she went back to help at the shelter. He would be over the moon, with so many people to love him.

The tears started to run down her cheeks again as she pictured him, curled up on a bed just like this one, while a girl the same age as her petted him gently.

Harry was pulling anxiously at his leash as Sam Ashcroft coaxed him to chase the ball. The children were so bouncy and excited, and it was just too much for him. Harry had had such a hard time recently — moving around all over the place, and having to get used to so many new people. He simply wasn't ready for three energetic children who wanted him to play all the time.

"Why won't he chase it?" Sam asked angrily. "I've been trying forever."

"Maybe he's tired," Luke suggested. "Mom's over there talking to that lady from school. We'd better tell her."

"But I don't want to go home!" Lily wailed, and Harry flinched at the noise.

Mrs. Ashcroft said good-bye to her friend and walked over to the children. "Come on, guys, we need to get home. Sally from the rescue shelter is coming to see how we're doing with Harry."

Harry plodded along the pavement with Luke, jumping when cars whooshed past. Everything seemed scary at the moment. He wished he could just curl up in his basket, and everyone would leave him alone. His ears were tensely pricked for the entire walk, and when a piece of litter blew in front of him, he gave a sharp, frightened little bark.

Mrs. Ashcroft looked at him worriedly, but she didn't say anything.

The children were even noisier than usual when they got home. After Lily had nearly run him over twice with her doll's stroller, Harry decided to take drastic action. He hid under the sofa. It was quiet, it was dark, and nobody could find him to make him chase balls, or jump into boxes, or even just hug him. He didn't want to be hugged right now.

The doorbell rang, and Harry shuddered as the children thundered down the hallway to the door.

"I just don't know where he could've gone," Mrs. Ashcroft was saying worriedly. "We came back from our walk about 20 minutes ago. He must have slipped away somewhere."

"Is he settling in well?" It was a familiar voice. Harry was sure he knew it. It wasn't Grace, but it made him think of her. He poked his nose out from under the sofa to hear better.

"There he is!" Lily shrieked, and Harry shot backward.

Lily crouched down to peer under the sofa, and Harry backed away from her. She swept her hand underneath, and called to him to come out. Harry barked anxiously. Why wouldn't they just leave him alone?

"Lily, stop that!" Mrs. Ashcroft said worriedly. "Now, Lily!"

Harry was still barking, a sharp, unhappy bark that sounded like a warning. *Leave me alone! Go away!*

Lily scrambled to her feet, her bottom lip wobbling. "I don't like it when he barks like that," she said tearfully.

Mrs. Ashcroft sighed, and looked at Sally. "I was hoping to be able to tell you he was starting to settle in," she said. "But I just don't think he is. The children have tried really hard, but I think we're a bit too much for him to take. He's a wonderful little dog, but he just doesn't seem very happy."

Sally nodded sadly. "I think you're right. I have a dog carrier in my car. I'm so sorry it hasn't worked out.

Hopefully we can find you another dog — one that's used to a busy house."

Mrs. Ashcroft and the children left Sally to coax Harry out, which she managed to do by being very quiet, and opening a package of dog treats.

Then it was back to the animal rescue shelter — again.

"He really is the boomerang dog, isn't he?" Sally sighed, as she and Mandy watched Harry eating his breakfast on Sunday morning.

"It's such a shame Grace couldn't take him home," Mandy said. "She built up such a wonderful relationship with him."

Sally nodded, then she smiled slowly.

"Of course! You've given me a great idea! I wonder if Grace and Danny are coming in today. I'm going to give their mom and dad a call."

She came back out of the reception area smiling. "They'll be here shortly. I can't wait to see Grace's reaction."

Mandy was frowning. "But I thought you'd decided that Harry loving Grace so much was keeping him from settling in with a new owner. Are you sure you want him to see her again?"

Sally nodded. "But I didn't tell you — the family moved. They wanted to adopt Harry, but he'd already gone to the Ashcrofts. They were going to think about another dog when they felt ready. And I've told them that the perfect dog has just arrived...."

Grace pushed open the door to the dogs' area, leading the way for Mom and Dad and Danny. Her hands felt sweaty, and slipped on the door handle. She was so nervous. Sally had said that a wonderful new dog had arrived, one who would be perfect for Grace and her family.

Why wasn't she happy?

All she could think of was Harry. She tried desperately to picture him with those other children, having a wonderful time. This other dog really needed a home, too.

"You all right?" Danny asked her, looking at her thoughtfully.

"I suppose," Grace whispered. "It just feels odd."

"I know." He sighed. "But this dog will be great, too."

Grace grabbed his arm. "Look!"

Sally was walking down the hallway, carrying a puppy in her arms. A Jack Russell puppy, white with brown patches, whose ears pricked up when he heard Grace's voice. He gave one joyful bark, and twisted right out of Sally's hold, leaping to the ground, his paws scratching the floor frantically as he raced toward them.

"Harry! It's Harry!" Grace scooped him up, and he licked her face delightedly, then generously leaned out of her arms to lick Danny, too. He'd missed Grace so much, and she'd come — she'd come back for him!

Sally grinned. "Told you I had the perfect dog...."

"I can't believe it," Grace whispered, hugging Harry tightly. "Thank you so much!" she told Sally.

Sally smiled at her. "I'm just glad he's found the right home at last. I don't think he'll be coming back to us again. But you have to do me one favor. Will you write to Beth, his old owner, for me? Tell her all about Harry's new home?"

"Of course!" Grace nodded eagerly.

Harry looked around to see Sally getting his basket and toys out of the cage and handing them to Danny. She gave Grace his leash. Harry's stubby little tail wagged delightedly as Grace clipped on the leash. He'd never seen Grace look this happy before. He gave her a hopeful look. If his basket and his toys were coming....

Grace was staring at him with shining eyes. "Oh, Harry! You're really coming home with us. We don't have to say good-bye this time."

"Harry, don't chew that pencil," Grace giggled. "Dogs aren't meant to eat pencils. It's not good for you."

She reached over to her nightstand. "Here — have a dog biscuit instead. But don't leave any crumbs on the comforter, okay? Mom's not sure about your being on my bed; we don't want to give her anything to complain about!"

Harry gnawed happily on the dog biscuit, letting Grace chat away. He loved it when she talked to him. Maybe after she'd finished this thing she was doing they could go to the park, with Danny, too. He gulped the last of the bone, and stretched out his paws. She was still writing. He'd take a little nap.

Grace looked down at him lovingly, curled up next to her teddy bear. She couldn't believe Harry had found a home at last — with her.

Dear Beth,

Sally gave me your address so I could write and tell you all about Harry. He has been living with us for two weeks now, and he is wonderful. (I know you know that already!) I really hope you're enjoying living in London, and you don't miss him too much.

Did Harry like smoky bacon treats when he lived with you? He stole a whole packet out of my brother's bag yesterday. Luckily Danny loves him so much that he went and got him another packet from the store. Mom was really angry, but it's okay — Harry wasn't sick.

Harry loves playing in our yard and going for walks, and he's very good at doing tricks now. He can shake hands, and roll over, and he'll almost stay, but not if you put a dog biscuit in front of him. We're still working on that one!

Lots of love,
Grace and Harry

The Runaway Puppy

Contents

For Phoebe

Chapter One
An Energetic Puppy

"Wait for me!" Sophie called after her twin brothers. She was pedaling as fast as she could, but they were so much bigger than she was, and they had gotten new mountain bikes for their birthday last month. There was no way she could catch up to them if they didn't slow down a bit. "Tom! Michael! Wait for me! Please!"

Tom and Michael circled around and hurtled back toward her, braking and pulling up in a cloud of dust.

"Come on, Sophie! You must be able to pedal a *bit* faster," Michael told her, laughing.

"Aw, now that's not fair, Mikey, she's only got little legs." Tom grinned at Sophie, and she scowled back.

"Can't we take a rest for a minute anyway?" she begged. "I want to watch the dogs, and this is the best place for that. I want to see if any of the ones I know are out for walks today."

"Yeah, I don't mind," Tom agreed.

Michael rolled his eyes. "Just for a minute. You're dog-mad, Sophie Martin!" he told her, grinning.

They wheeled their bikes out of the way of the path, and then slumped on a bench. All three of them stared out across the grass, which was packed with dogs and their owners. This was definitely the best place for dog-watching: raised up on a little hill, they could see all the way around.

"Look, Sophie, there's that Red Setter you like." Michael pointed at a dog scampering around on one of the paths, its dark reddish coat gleaming in the sunlight.

Sophie giggled as she watched him running around in circles, and nosing at sticks. His owner was trying to get him to fetch a ball, but the big dog was not interested.

Tom sighed. "If I had a dog, I'd train

it an awful lot better than that one. Poor thing doesn't know whether it's coming or going."

"I don't think it's very easy to train a dog," Sophie said.

"Of course it isn't," Tom agreed. "That's why there are so many badly behaved dogs around. People can't be bothered to train their dogs properly, and they just let them do whatever they want because it's easier than getting them to behave."

"Okay, if you could have any dog you want, what would you have?" Michael asked. "Mom and Dad keep saying that one day we can. Dad didn't say no last time I asked."

Tom whistled through his teeth. "Nothing small and yappy. A dog you could take on proper walks. Maybe a Dalmatian."

"Mmm, I could go for a Dalmatian. Or a golden retriever," Michael mused. "Wouldn't it be great to get a dog now, just before summer vacation? We'd have all summer to go for really long walks."

Tom nodded. "Don't get your hopes up. What would you have, Sophie?"

Sophie was staring back down the path that they'd come up. "I'd have a Labrador. But a chocolate one, like Buttons. I *think* that's her coming up the path now. Oh, dear...."

"What did she do this time?" Tom asked.

Sophie put her hand over her mouth to stifle her giggles, as the chocolate-brown Labrador puppy danced around her owner, tangling him in her leash.

"Whoops," Tom muttered, and Michael bobbed up from the bench to see what was going on.

"Ow, that must've hurt. Do you think we should go and help?"

Buttons was standing on the path, looking down at her owner in confusion.

What on earth are you doing down there? she seemed to be saying. Her owner unwrapped her leash from his ankles grimly, and started to heave himself up out of the bush.

Sophie looked at Tom and Michael. "We probably should, but Buttons's owner is so grumpy, he might yell at us."

"His name is Mr. Jenkins," Tom told her. "I heard one of his neighbors talking to him when we walked past his house the other day."

Michael nodded. "I think Sophie's right. He's probably hoping no one saw. We'd better be looking the other way when he comes past."

All three children stared innocently at the grass toward the lake, pretending not to have seen Buttons trip up Mr. Jenkins.

"Good morning!" Michael called politely, as the old man walked by, trying to hold Buttons back to heel. Mr. Jenkins lived on the next road across from the Martins, and his yard backed up into theirs, so they saw him quite often. Their mom always said hello when she passed him.

"Hmmph," Mr. Jenkins grunted, and stomped on past.

"You see! So grumpy!" Sophie whispered, as he disappeared down the path.

"Yes, but I'd be grumpy, too, if I'd just fallen in a bush," Tom pointed out.

Buttons appreciated them saying hello, anyway. She looked back and barked in a friendly way as Mr. Jenkins hurried her along. She liked those children. They always smiled when they saw her, and the girl had once asked to pet her. Mr. Jenkins had let her, and she'd said how beautiful Buttons was and scratched behind her ears.

"Come on, Buttons," Mr. Jenkins grumbled, and Buttons sighed. He was angry with her again. She hadn't *meant* to trip him up. There were so many good smells on the field, and she couldn't help it if they were on different sides of the path. She'd wanted to investigate them all, and the silly leash had gotten tangled in his legs. She much preferred to run along without a leash. Especially if there were squirrels.

They were coming to the part of the field with the trees now, and there was bound to be a squirrel. Buttons looked up and barked hopefully.

"No, I'm not letting you off your

leash, silly dog," Mr. Jenkins told her, but he patted her lovingly on the head at the same time, and she knew he wasn't angry anymore. "No, because you'll be in the next county before I catch up with you. I'm sorry, Buttons girl, we need to head home. My legs aren't what they used to be, especially when I've been dragged through a bush. Come on, home now."

Buttons whined sadly. She understood some words, and *home* was one of them. Not home already! It felt like it hadn't been a very long walk at all. She wanted lots of walks—in fact, a whole day of walks, with a few quick naps and a couple of big meals in between, would be perfect.

"Look, Mom, Buttons is in her yard again." Sophie nudged her mother's arm as they walked past Mr. Jenkins's house. Summer vacation had started, and it was so hot that they were going to cool off at the pool. "She keeps scratching at the fence like she wants to get out. She was doing that yesterday, when I went past on my way to say good-bye to Rachel. I heard her barking a lot when I was out in the yard, too."

Mom stopped and looked over the fence at Buttons. "Have you seen Mr. Jenkins lately?" she asked Sophie. "I haven't, and I usually see him in the store every so often."

Sophie shook her head. "Not since that day in the park a couple of weeks ago, when Buttons tripped him up. I definitely haven't seen him since school finished, and that's a whole week."

She sighed. Only one week of summer vacation gone. She should to be looking forward to another five weeks off from school, but yesterday her best friend, Rachel, had gone to Ireland to stay with her family for the summer. Sophie couldn't imagine what she was going to do all summer, without Rachel's house to hang out at. She was sick of Michael and Tom already. Not only were they her big brothers, so they thought they could always boss her around, but they were each other's best friends. They didn't want their little sister tagging

271

along the whole time. She and Rachel had promised to keep in touch by email and send each other lots of fun postcards and things. But it wasn't the same as having your best friend living just around the corner.

Buttons looked up at Sophie and barked hopefully. *Walk? Please?* she begged. She knew Sophie, who often spoke to her when she went past. Buttons could sometimes hear her in the yard, too. Sophie had always sounded friendly.

"Poor Buttons. She looks really sad," Sophie said, wishing she could pet her. She knew Buttons was friendly, but Mom had made her promise not to pet dogs without asking the owner first.

"Now that I think about it, I did see Mr. Jenkins in the store last week, and he was walking with a cane," Mom said slowly. "I wonder if he hasn't been able to take Buttons for walks, and that's why she's scratching. She wants to get out."

"Sorry, Buttons, we're going swimming, or else we'd take you for a walk. Look, she knows what we're saying! Her ears just drooped, and she isn't wagging her tail anymore," Sophie said as she waved good-bye.

Buttons stared after them with big, sad brown eyes. She hadn't been on a proper walk in a long time. Mr. Jenkins was very good about letting her in and out of the house whenever she wanted, but he just didn't seem to want to walk her right now. The yard was big—it went all around the house from front to back—but it wasn't the same as walks. Then Buttons whined sadly, and scratched at the fence again. She thought she might be able to go for a walk by herself,

if she could only get over this fence.
Or under it.

"Buttons! Buttons!" She could hear
Mr. Jenkins calling, and her ears
pricked up immediately. Maybe he
was feeling better, and he wanted to
go for a walk. She ran to the back
door, which Mr. Jenkins was holding
open for her.

"There you
are! You've
been out
a while,
Buttons."
Mr. Jenkins
stooped down
to pat her,
holding tight
to his cane.

Buttons looked up at him hopefully, and then looked over at her leash, which was hanging on a hook above Mr. Jenkins's boots. She gave an excited little bark, and wagged her tail so fast it blurred.

"Oh, Buttons, I wish we could. I wish we could, poor little girl. Soon, I promise."

Buttons's tail sagged, and she trailed slowly into the living room to curl up on her cushion next to Mr. Jenkins's chair. He sat down beside her, and petted her head lovingly. Buttons licked his hand. She adored Mr. Jenkins, even though he couldn't always take her for walks.

Chapter Two
A Surprise Meeting

"If you're going along the canal path, you must be careful," Mom warned them. "Especially you, Sophie. No going close to the edge, promise?"

"I'm not a baby, Mom!" Sophie complained. Then she softened. "Okay, I promise to be careful."

"All right then. Tom and Michael, you'll keep an eye on her, won't you?

Don't leave her behind."

Sophie's older brothers nodded, eager to get out on their ride, even if it did mean taking Sophie, too.

It was a beautiful, sunny Saturday afternoon, and Mom and Dad were repainting the kitchen, so it was definitely a good time to be out of the house. The canal path was the Martin family's other favorite place to go on walks and bike rides. They were lucky that it wasn't far from where they lived.

Despite what they'd said to Mom, Michael and Tom couldn't resist speeding off ahead. Every so often one of them would check that Sophie was okay, and she was—she quite liked riding along on her own anyway. It meant she could stop and talk to the tabby cat sitting on the fence—he let her pet him today—and admire the butterflies on a lilac tree that grew on the corner of the canal bank. She could do all these things without the boys telling her to hurry up all the time.

Sophie pedaled along, keeping away from the edge like Mom had told her to. The canal was beautiful, especially with the sun sparkling on it like it was today, but beneath the glitter the water was deep and dark. She rounded the bend, expecting to see Tom and Michael, but instead she saw a familiar-looking dog.

Buttons!

The pretty little Labrador was sniffing around at the water's edge. Sophie cycled closer, smiling at Buttons's big chocolate paws, and her floppy ears.

Sophie looked around for Mr. Jenkins, but she couldn't see him anywhere, and she had a feeling that Buttons had run off. She wasn't old enough to be off the leash—and she wasn't; it was trailing in the mud. Buttons must've pulled it out of Mr. Jenkins's hand.

Buttons hadn't noticed Sophie. She was watching a stick that was floating down the canal, and wondering whether she could reach it, if she just leaned over a little. It looked like such a good one—big and long and really muddy—and it was really close. She leaned out over the water. If she could just get the end of it in her teeth.... But it was still a bit too far away. She tried again, reaching further out.

"Buttons! Don't!" Sophie called. "You'll fall!"

Surprised by Sophie's shout, Buttons stepped back quickly. But the edge of the canal bank was muddy and slippery, and her paws skidded. Panicking, she tried to scramble back up the bank, but she was sliding further in, and she couldn't stop herself.

Sophie flung down her bike, and raced to grab Buttons's leash. She caught it just as the puppy's front paws slid into the water. Sophie pulled hard on the leash, leaning back—Buttons might be little, but she was heavy. Sophie wondered if Buttons just might accidentally pull her into the water, too, but she finally hauled Buttons back on to the bank.

She hugged the shivering puppy tightly. "It's all right, Buttons. Oh, dear, your paws are all wet. It's okay, don't worry," Sophie murmured soothingly, trying to calm her down. Buttons buried her nose in Sophie's shirt, breathing in her smell. Sophie had saved her!

"Buttons! Buttons!" Mr. Jenkins was hurrying up, walking as fast as he could with his cane. "What happened, did she fall in?" he asked worriedly. "I saw you pulling her leash. Are you okay? Is she all right?"

He leaned down slowly to pet Buttons, and she pressed herself against his legs, making frightened little whimpering noises. "Oh, Buttons, you silly girl, what have you been doing?"

He looked up and smiled apologetically at Sophie. "She pulled her leash out of my hand and raced off. It's the first time we've been for a walk in a while. Buttons is overexcited to be out again."

Sophie smiled back at him, though her heart was still thumping. It had been a scary moment. "She didn't go right in. She was just starting to slip, but I grabbed her leash before she did more than get her paws wet."

"Sophie! Are you okay?" Tom and Michael had come riding up, and they looked worried. The little sister they were supposed to be watching was sitting on the canal bank with a wet dog, her bike flung down on the grass.

"Were you playing around by the

water? Mom said to stay away from the edge!" Tom shouted.

"Of course I wasn't!" Sophie said indignantly.

Mr. Jenkins looked at the boys. "Your sister stopped Buttons from falling in. She's a hero." He slowly straightened up. "I think we were ambitious with this walk, Buttons."

"Would you like me to walk Buttons home for you?" Sophie asked.

Mr. Jenkins smiled. "It's very kind of you to offer, but you weren't going home yet, were you? I don't want to take you out of your way."

"That's all right. Isn't it?" Sophie asked Tom and Michael. "Mom wouldn't mind if I went back, would she?"

The boys exchanged glances. "We'll come, too," said Tom. "That way, we can wheel your bike while you're walking Buttons."

"Oh! I'd forgotten my bike," Sophie admitted. "I was too excited about getting to walk such a beautiful puppy."

"She is pretty, isn't she?" Mr. Jenkins agreed, as they all started to walk home slowly. "Bit of a handful at the moment, though. She's got so much energy."

Buttons was darting here and there, sniffing excitedly at the scents of other dogs and people. Sophie laughed as she followed her, but she could see that such a bouncy little dog would be hard work for Mr. Jenkins.

"I really need to take her to some dog-training classes, but we just haven't been able to get out much recently. Soon though," Mr. Jenkins added, as he watched Buttons racing about.

"Where did you get her?" Sophie asked, wishing she could have a beautiful chocolate-colored dog like Buttons.

"She came from a breeder who lives over on the other side of town. I got my last two dogs from him as well, but they were golden Labradors. Buttons is the first chocolate one I've had."

"Buttons is such a perfect name for a chocolate Labrador," Sophie told him, giggling.

"Ah, that wasn't me. It was my granddaughter Phoebe's idea. She thought it was really funny."

"Does she live around here?" Sophie asked. "I don't know anyone named Phoebe at school."

"No." Mr. Jenkins shook his head sadly. "My son had to move with work earlier in the year. They live in California now. I try and get over to see them, but I do miss her."

Sophie nodded. "My grandpa lives in Arizona; we don't see him much either. And my nana and my other grandpa live in Hawaii, really far away. We call them lots, but it's not the same as seeing them."

Mr. Jenkins sighed. "Not at all. Phoebe hasn't even seen Buttons yet; I got her six weeks ago. I've sent some photos."

Buttons was enjoying following all

the delicious smells, and with Sophie holding her leash, she could go as fast as she liked. She was sure that there had been a mouse along here recently. It had gone this way, then back over here—oh! She was almost at the water's edge. She stepped back, whining. She loved to look at the water, but she didn't want to be in it.

Buttons looked up gratefully at Sophie, who was gripping her leash tightly. She was very glad that Sophie had been there to pull her out before. She knew she shouldn't have run off from Mr. Jenkins like that, but they'd been going so slowly. Still, she wouldn't do it again. She wouldn't run away ever again....

Chapter Three
Buttons in Trouble

Sophie and the boys said good-bye to Mr. Jenkins at the door. The old man was very grateful, and told Sophie that she was quick-thinking and helpful, and she reminded him of his granddaughter.

"That's all right," Sophie said, blushing, as she took her bike back from Tom. "I'm glad I was there to catch her."

Sophie watched as Mr. Jenkins let himself and Buttons into the house, then she and the boys pedaled home excitedly.

Luckily Mom and Dad were taking a break from painting, so they were able to listen to Sophie when she dashed in, full of her news.

"Good job, Sophie." Her dad smiled, but then he looked worried. "I hope you were careful, though. A big dog like a Labrador could've easily pulled you in, too."

"Oh, no, Dad, Buttons is only little—she's just a puppy," Sophie explained. Then she noticed that Michael and Tom were making faces at her behind Dad's back and added, "And Tom and Mike were only a bit ahead of me; they'd have pulled me out if I *had* fallen in."

Her mom shuddered. "Well, thank goodness you didn't."

"I think Soph deserves an ice-cream cone," her dad put in. "I'd like one, too, after all that painting. Want to run down to the ice-cream shop?"

"Oooh, yes!" And Sophie gave him a hug, being careful of the paint.

When they were all sitting around in the yard eating their ice cream, Sophie said thoughtfully, "Mom, do you think Mr. Jenkins would like me to walk Buttons for him while his leg's bad? He said he'd have to take it easy for a couple more days, but I think a dog like Buttons needs walks *every* day."

Mom and Dad exchanged glances,

and Mom sighed. "You're right, Sophie. She would need lots of walks, a young energetic dog like that. Probably Mr. Jenkins could use some help. We don't want to make him feel like we're interfering, or that we think he can't handle it. If he asked, it would be different...."

"I bet he won't ask," Tom said, through a mouthful of ice cream. "He's not that sort of person."

"Well, if I see him, I'll try and feel him out," Mom suggested. "Okay? A compromise."

Sophie nodded reluctantly. Poor Buttons. It looked like she was going to be stuck in the yard again for a while.

Buttons followed Mr. Jenkins into the house a little sadly. It had been fun walking with Sophie. Buttons tried hard not to pull on her leash with Mr. Jenkins; she could tell it was hard for him to walk. She forgot sometimes. It was hard to remember to be careful when she saw something she just had to chase. With Sophie, she had felt it was all right to be her bouncy self, and Buttons hoped she would see her again soon. Maybe Mr. Jenkins would take her on a walk tomorrow.

But he didn't. On Monday morning, Buttons hopefully brought him her leash, just in case, but he was sitting in his chair, recovering from the effort of getting down the stairs.

"I'm sorry, Buttons. Not today."
He sighed as he took her leash and
heaved himself up. "You go and have
a run around the yard, that's a good
girl. And I'll put your food out for you
in a minute."

Buttons could feel him watching
her as she skittered off into the yard.
He looked anxious, and she wondered
what was wrong. He was still holding
her leash, looking at it sadly.

Buttons looked around the yard and gave a little whine. She would prefer a walk, but the yard was better than nothing. She was sniffing thoughtfully through the flower bed by the fence, when she came across a little hole under a bush. It was just large enough to get her nose into, but the loose dirt made her back out quickly, sneezing and shaking her muzzle.

Once she'd stopped pawing at her nose, Buttons sat and looked at the hole, with her head to one side. It was only a small hole. But she was sure it could be bigger. If there was a hole under the fence, she could go for a walk by herself. Without her leash! Buttons crouched down, and started to scrape at the dirt with one paw....

The hole took a while to dig, but no one noticed what Buttons was doing because of the bush. It was a perfect cover.

Late the next afternoon, Buttons wriggled and squirmed her way out under the fence, and stood in the street, looking around in delight. She could go wherever she wanted! She sniffed the air eagerly. Which way should she go first? The most delicious smells wafted past her and she pattered off down the street, looking around curiously.

On a wall two houses down from Mr. Jenkins's house, a black cat was snoozing in the sun, its tail dangling invitingly down the side of the wall. Buttons trotted up to it and barked. She wanted to run. It would be even better if she could chase something! She didn't know that chasing cats wasn't allowed—there was just something about the cat that made her want to bark at it....

The cat woke up with a start, and meowed frantically, its tail puffing out and all the fur standing up along its back.

Buttons stood at the bottom of the wall, barking excitedly, and the cat hissed and spat at her.

"Go away! Bad dog!" A woman was hurrying down the path, waving a trowel angrily.

Buttons didn't know what she'd done wrong, but she knew what bad dog meant. She slunk away with her tail between her legs, just in time to see Mr. Jenkins standing at his gate, looking around for her worriedly.

"Is this your dog?" the cat's owner demanded. "She's been terrorizing my poor Felix. You should keep her in your yard!"

"I'm sorry." Mr. Jenkins limped out and caught Buttons by the collar. "I don't know how she got out. Has she hurt the cat?"

"Well, no," the lady admitted. "But he's terrified!" And she stomped back around the side of her house, carrying Felix and muttering about badly-behaved dogs.

"Oh, Buttons." Mr. Jenkins sighed.

Buttons looked up at him apologetically, giving her tail a hopeful little wag. She hadn't been that naughty, had she?

Mr. Jenkins didn't know about the hole Buttons had dug under the fence. He thought that the mailman must have let her out, or the paper boy. He put a note on the gate reminding people to shut it carefully, and kept Buttons in for the rest of the day.

The next day, Sophie went out to send a postcard to Rachel. The mailbox was on the next street—the street where Mr. Jenkins and Buttons lived. Sophie was hoping she might see Buttons on the way; she was sure she'd heard her barking from her yard. Mr. Jenkins might be in the yard, too—Mom hadn't asked him about Sophie walking Buttons yet, and Sophie was tempted to ask him herself.

On her way back, Sophie was just coming around the corner toward Mr. Jenkins's house, when she heard a scuffling noise, loud barking, and someone shouting.

Sophie hurried around the corner. Buttons was out! The little dog was standing with her front paws on the wall, barking at a black cat who was on the top, trying to claw at Buttons's nose.

"Buttons, no!" Sophie cried, running over. "You can't chase cats!"

The black cat jumped from the wall into the safety of a tree. Buttons barked one last flurry of barks, then looked guiltily at Sophie. She'd gotten in trouble yesterday, but she'd forgotten. Cats were just so tempting!

"Do you know this dog? Can you grab her collar, please?" A woman was hurrying up the path. "I need to take her back to her owner. This is the third time she's chased my cat; she was out this morning, too."

Sophie caught Buttons's collar, and patted her gently to try and calm her down. Buttons wriggled, so Sophie picked her up instead, and the puppy snuggled gratefully into her arms.

"Be careful!" the cat's owner said anxiously. "She's snappy! Vicious little thing."

Sophie looked at the woman in surprise. Buttons? Sophie was sure she wasn't vicious, just a bit naughty.

The woman came out of her yard, looking worriedly up at her cat, and opened Mr. Jenkins's gate. "Could you take her back? She seems to behave for you. I need to talk to Mr. Jenkins, because this is getting silly."

Sophie followed her, almost wishing she hadn't gone out to send her postcard. She was glad she'd been able to catch Buttons—the little dog could have been hurt if she'd run into the road—but she didn't want to be in the middle of an argument between Mr. Jenkins and his neighbor.

Mr. Jenkins answered the door, and he looked horrified when he saw them. "Mrs. Lane! Sophie! Oh, Buttons, not again...."

"Again," Mrs. Lane said grimly. "You promised me this morning you wouldn't let her out!"

"I really am sorry, Mrs. Lane. I've

got someone coming to block up the hole under the fence later on, and I've kept Buttons shut in ever since I found it. She must've climbed out of the window." He gestured at an open window, and Sophie noticed that the flowers underneath looked rather squashed.

"If this happens again, I'll have to report you to animal control," Mrs. Lane said angrily. Then she sighed. "I'm sorry. I don't mean to be rude. But you're just not keeping her properly under control. She's a little terror!"

Mr. Jenkins frowned. "I can only apologize, and promise you it won't happen again." He leaned wearily against the door frame.

"Please make sure that it doesn't."

Mrs. Lane looked at him and her voice softened. "Are you all right, Mr. Jenkins? Would you like me to call your doctor? You don't look very well."

Mr. Jenkins stood up very straight. "I'm perfectly fine, thank you," he said coldly. "Sophie, could you pass Buttons to me, please?"

Sophie handed Buttons over a little reluctantly. Mrs. Lane was right—he didn't look well, and she was worried Buttons was too heavy for him to carry. But she didn't dare say so. "'Bye, Mr. Jenkins; 'bye, Buttons," she whispered.

Mrs. Lane stalked back down the path, and Sophie followed her, looking back to see Mr. Jenkins closing the window, and Buttons standing next to him now, with her paws on the windowsill—Sophie guessed the puppy was standing on a chair—staring sadly after her. "See you soon, Buttons!" she whispered. Maybe next time she'd ask about being allowed to walk her.

That night, Sophie sat curled up in bed, staring out of her window. Her room was at the back of the house, and she could see the big tree in Mr. Jenkins's yard and his house beyond. Buttons was in there. At least, Sophie hoped she was. She'd been lying in bed, thinking about how she'd see Mr. Jenkins tomorrow and ask him about walking Buttons, but then she'd had an awful thought.

What if the little dog had already gotten out again? Sophie had a horrible feeling that if Buttons could dig one hole under the fence, then it wouldn't be long before she'd make another one. And this time she'd be in *real* trouble.

I should have been brave enough to ask Mr. Jenkins about walking her, she thought miserably, one tear trickling down her cheek. If Buttons didn't get walked, she'd get out by herself. That lady had said she'd call animal control if Buttons chased her cat again.

"Sophie! Why are you still awake? It's really late." Her mom was looking around the door. "Oh, Sophie, what's wrong?" She came in and sat on the bed. "You're crying!"

"Mom, what would happen to a dog if somebody called animal control about her?" Sophie asked worriedly.

Her mom put an arm around her. "I—I don't know, Sophie. Is this about Buttons?" Sophie had told her what had happened earlier.

"Mrs. Lane said she'd call animal control. They'd take Buttons away. I know they would. She'd get put in the animal shelter."

Her mom sighed. "I know it's hard to accept, but that might not be a bad thing...."

"Mom!" Sophie looked shocked.

"You've been saying that Mr. Jenkins can't walk Buttons enough, Sophie. She's only going to get bigger, and stronger. She's not an old man's dog. She's such a sweet puppy, and she'd probably be adopted by a nice family."

"But she loves Mr. Jenkins!" Sophie told her anxiously. "You can see from the way she looks at him. And he's lonely, with all his family far away. He needs her, Mom." She didn't add that if Buttons got a new home, she'd never see her again. But she couldn't help *thinking* it.

Sophie's mom nodded sadly. "I know. I'm sorry, Sophie. I just don't think there's a right answer to all of this." She stood up. "Try to go to sleep, okay?"

Sophie nodded. But after her mom had gone, she went back to looking out the window, and thinking about Buttons. "Be good, Buttons!" she murmured, as she finally lay down to sleep.

Chapter Four
The Rescue Mission

Buttons had just finished her breakfast, and she was playing with one of the new chew toys Mr. Jenkins had gotten to keep her entertained, when she heard a terrible, sliding crash. She dashed into the hallway, where the noise seemed to have come from.

Mr. Jenkins was lying in a heap at the bottom of the stairs.

Buttons howled in shock and fright. Her owner wasn't moving. It looked as though he'd tripped over his cane on the way down the stairs. Miserably, she waited for him to get up.

He didn't.

After waiting for a few minutes, staring worriedly at his closed eyes and pale face, Buttons nosed him gently. Was he asleep?

Mr. Jenkins groaned; Buttons jumped back. That wasn't a good noise.

"Buttons...," he muttered. "Good girl. I'll get up in a minute." But as he tried to move, Mr. Jenkins collapsed again. "No, I can't." He was silent for a moment, breathing fast. "Buttons, go get help. Go on...." His voice died away, and his eyes closed again, as Buttons watched him anxiously.

He didn't stir, even when Buttons licked his face, very gently.

Buttons whined. He'd said to get help, but she wasn't sure what he meant. Sophie! She would get Sophie. Buttons was sure she would know what to do.

Buttons backed away from Mr. Jenkins slowly, and looked at the front door. It was closed. She trotted down the hallway and into the kitchen. The back door was shut, too. She nudged it hopefully. Mr. Jenkins had let her out first thing—perhaps he hadn't quite closed it? But it was shut, and pawing at it did nothing.

She walked back up the hallway. Mr. Jenkins hadn't moved. People weren't meant to be that still. She had to get out and find Sophie! Buttons stood by the door and barked loudly, hoping that someone would open it for her, but no one did.

She stared at the door for a minute, then went into the living room. Buttons eyed the window.

She knew she wasn't supposed to do this. Mr. Jenkins had said no, very angrily, and that she must never do it again.

But what else was she supposed to do? No one had come when she called. The doors were all shut. It was the only way out, and Mr. Jenkins needed help.

Buttons clambered on to the armchair and up on to the top, so that her front paws were on the windowsill. Then she stuck her nose through the window. It was only open a crack. Mr. Jenkins liked fresh air, and he always had the windows open, but he had almost shut this one because of the time she'd climbed out the window. But when she pushed with her nose, the window opened more.

Now she could get her ears through—although it was a squeeze and it hurt. Buttons wriggled her shoulders as if she were shaking water out of her fur, and scratched and scrambled and finally tumbled out the window, landing clumsily in the flower bed underneath.

She wasn't excited by the idea of a trip, like she'd been yesterday. Now she wanted to be curled up next to Mr. Jenkins's armchair, his hand petting her ears, watching one of those delicious food programs on the television.

Buttons headed for her little hole under the fence, but when she wriggled under the bush, it wasn't there! She lay there staring at the fence, whimpering in confusion. Brand-new boards had been nailed across the bottom, and her hole had been completely blocked up. She'd gone through all that trouble to get into the yard, and now she couldn't get out.

Suddenly Buttons's ears pricked up. She could hear Sophie! Sophie was in her yard on the other side of the back fence. She wriggled out from under the bush, barking loudly as she ran to the other end of the yard.

"Hi, Buttons!" Sophie called back, laughing, and Buttons barked louder. Sophie didn't understand! She thought Buttons was just barking to be friendly, like she sometimes did. She would have to get out of the yard and go and get Sophie. She gave a few more loud barks, then scampered back to look at the gate.

She had tried to open it before, and it hadn't worked, but she had been smaller then. She would try again. She scratched at it, but not much happened. It shook a little, but that was all. Buttons took a few steps back and looked up. That silvery part sticking out at the top was what made it open, she was sure. It clicked and rattled when people came in. If she could pull it across, the gate would open. And she thought she was tall enough now, if she really stretched.

Luckily for Buttons, the bolt was old and loose, but not rusty, and when she pulled at it with her strong, sharp, young teeth, it slid back easily enough. The gate opened, and Buttons sat in front of it, looking out at the street in amazement. She had done it!

Now all she had to do was find Sophie.

Buttons trotted out into the street. Then she stared back at the house, one last time, hoping the front door would open, and Mr. Jenkins would come out, saying he was all right now. She wouldn't even mind if he scolded her for opening the gate.

But the door stayed firmly shut. Buttons looked up and down the road. She needed to find Sophie's house. Maybe she could sniff her out.

"Naughty dog!" someone shouted, and Buttons raced off. She knew that voice—the angry lady with the cat. She wanted Buttons to come back, but Buttons wasn't going to let anyone stop her now.

Buttons sped around the corner, looking back over her shoulder anxiously. No one was following. Good. She looked at the houses on either side of the road, and her tail drooped. How was she supposed to know which house was Sophie's? She was sure it had to be here somewhere. But figuring out exactly which house lined up with hers was going to be tough.

Perhaps she could call Sophie? She barked hopefully, then louder and louder again. Nothing happened.

Buttons sat down in the middle of the pavement and howled. She would never find Sophie.

"Buttons!"

Sophie came running toward her, followed by Tom and Michael. "I told you I heard her barking. There *is* something wrong, I know there is. Oh, no, I hope she hasn't been chasing that cat."

Buttons ran up to them, wagging her tail gratefully. She'd almost given up.

"We'd better take her back," Tom said. "Grab her collar, Sophie; we don't want her to run into the road."

But when Sophie tried to grab her collar, Buttons backed away.

"What's the matter, Buttons?" Sophie asked, feeling confused.

"She looks upset," Michael commented. "She isn't wagging her tail anymore. She isn't hurt, is she?"

Sophie crouched down and tried to

call the puppy over. "Here, Buttons, come on. Good girl." But Buttons whimpered, and looked anxiously down the street.

Sophie frowned. "I think she wants us to follow her. Come on! Show me, good dog, Buttons." And Sophie grabbed Tom and Michael by the hand and dragged them after her.

Buttons ran along in front of them, turning every few steps to check that they were following.

"I hope something hasn't happened to Mr. Jenkins," Michael muttered.

"What do you mean?" Sophie asked in an anxious voice.

"I can't think of why else she'd be so desperate for us to follow her," Michael explained reluctantly.

"Let's go faster," said Sophie, speeding up. "He looked awful when I took Buttons back yesterday."

They reached the house, panting, and Buttons pushed open the gate. Then she ran to the door, and paced back and forth between the door and the open window, whining. *Hurry, hurry!* she tried to tell them. *Let me in! You have to help him!*

Sophie rang the bell, but she didn't really expect anyone to answer it.

Buttons barked, sounding more and more desperate, and Tom pulled out his phone. "Do you think we should call the police?" he asked. "Or try the neighbors?"

"Shhhh!" Sophie said suddenly. "Listen. I can hear something."

Faintly, from inside the house, she could hear a voice. Even Buttons stopped barking. She listened, too, and she heard Mr. Jenkins saying, "Help! Buttons, are you there? Sophie, is that you?"

"He's calling for help!" Sophie gasped. She fumbled with the door handle, her fingers slipping. She was sure it hadn't been locked earlier.

"Not the police, an ambulance," Tom muttered, when Sophie had gotten the door open and he saw Mr. Jenkins lying at the foot of the stairs. "Don't move him!" he called to Sophie, who was kneeling beside the old man, her hand on Buttons's collar.

"I won't," Sophie said. "Mr. Jenkins, Buttons found us. Did you send her to find us? She's so clever; she made us follow her."

Mr. Jenkins looked up at her, smiling a little. "I knew she'd get help," he whispered. "Good dog, Buttons."

And Buttons licked his cheek very, very gently.

Chapter Five
Taking Care of Buttons

By the time the ambulance arrived, Mr. Jenkins was looking a little better. There was a touch of color in his cheeks. Buttons sat next to him, watching over him and every so often licking his hand.

The paramedics were impressed that Buttons had found Sophie, Tom, and Michael.

They petted her soft fur, and said how clever she was.

Mr. Jenkins smiled, then his face fell. "Buttons! What's going to happen to her? There's no one to take her!"

"We can arrange for her to go to the shelter for you, for a while," one of the paramedics suggested gently.

"No, no, she'd hate that...." Mr. Jenkins stared at Buttons.

Buttons whimpered, not knowing what was wrong.

"Careful now," the paramedic warned, trying to soothe the old man. "Don't get yourself upset."

"Tom, can't you call Mom and Dad?" Sophie begged. "We could take Buttons; I'm sure they'd say yes if we explained what happened."

Mr. Jenkins nodded gratefully. "That would be wonderful."

Tom grabbed his phone out of his pocket. Sophie watched nervously as he explained everything to Mom. "She said to bring her back with us," he said at last, smiling. "She wasn't sure, but she said okay."

"Go with Sophie, Buttons," Mr. Jenkins whispered, as the paramedics carried his stretcher down the path. "That's a good girl."

The ambulance sped away with its red lights flashing, and Buttons whimpered as she stared after it, watching until it disappeared around the corner. Then she looked up trustingly at Sophie. Mr. Jenkins had said to go with her, so she would.

Just then, Mrs. Lane, Mr. Jenkins's neighbor, came hurrying down the street. She had seen the ambulance and looked worried.

"Oh my goodness, was that Mr. Jenkins?" she asked the children, and when they nodded, she dropped her shopping bag, and her face went pale. "I knew I should have made him see a doctor," she said. "But he was so stubborn. Oh! The dog! What will we do with her?"

"We're taking her home with us," Sophie said firmly.

Mrs. Lane looked surprised, but rather relieved. "I can't possibly take her, you know. She chases Felix," she said very firmly.

Tom and Michael carried Buttons's things out of the house, and Sophie clipped on her leash. Mr. Jenkins had said to take everything they needed, and given them his house key to lock up afterward.

"Don't let her get out," Mrs. Lane advised as she stood watching.

Sophie, Tom, and Michael smiled, and didn't say anything, but as soon as they were around the corner— the boys with baskets and bowls and Sophie holding Buttons's leash and a big bag of dog food—they exchanged glances.

"She really doesn't like Buttons, does she," Tom muttered. "I'm glad Buttons didn't get left with her. She'd have been down at the animal shelter before she could blink."

"Buttons was only getting out and being naughty because she hadn't been walked, but that wasn't Mr. Jenkins's fault," Sophie said loyally.

Sophie's mom was standing at the gate watching for them. "Oh my goodness," she muttered, as she saw everything the boys were carrying. "Look at all that stuff!"

Buttons looked up at her worried face and whimpered. Everyone was angry at the moment, and Mr. Jenkins had gone away. She raised her head to the sky and howled.

"You'd better bring her in," Mom said, sighing.

Sophie coaxed Buttons in, and the boys carried all the things into the kitchen, putting them down next to their dad, who looked rather surprised to find a dog eyeing his sandwich enviously.

Dad shook his head, smiling a little. "Looks like you three got your wish, even if it is only for a week or two. Because that's all it is," he added firmly. "She's going back to Mr. Jenkins, so don't get too fond of her."

It was easy to promise that they wouldn't get too fond of Buttons, but Sophie adored her already and couldn't imagine life without her. Watching her every day wasn't hard work, as Dad had warned them. Tom borrowed a DVD on dog training from the library, and Sophie and her two brothers started to teach her to walk,

338

heel, sit, and stay. They'd always thought Buttons was naughty, because whenever they saw her she'd slipped her leash or tripped someone. When they'd first taken her for walks, Sophie had held on to her leash tightly, convinced that Buttons would try to run off. Although she did pull at her leash a bit, she didn't run away at all. And she was great with the obedience training.

"Labradors are very clever," Dad said, after he'd watched admiringly as they put Buttons through her paces for him. She'd even sat for a whole minute with a dog biscuit between her paws, until Sophie told her she was allowed to eat it.

Buttons was happy, too. She had

been very confused that first day, with a new house and a new yard and new people, even if her own basket and her bowls were there. And she had missed Mr. Jenkins terribly. Everywhere smelled different and strange, and she followed Sophie around as though she was glued to her.

On Saturday night, Mom had looked at her sad little face and big black eyes, and sighed. "I suppose she's going to have to sleep in your room, Sophie. But not on your bed!" she added, as Sophie rushed to hug her.

Buttons still thought about Mr. Jenkins, but she was happy living with a family who had as much energy as she did. It was the walks that made things so different. An early-morning quick run before breakfast with Sophie. Sometimes a trip down to the store during the day. And then a long walk later on. Up to the field, or along the canal. A week after she'd come home with them, the whole family went in the car to the woods a few miles from town, and Buttons had a wonderful time chasing imaginary rabbits.

That evening when they got home, Sophie sent Rachel an email. She had to type rather slowly, with Buttons sitting on her lap and staring curiously at the computer.

```
To: Rachel
From: Sophie                    ⫴ Attachment:
Subject: Our new dog?             Buttons.jpg

Hi Rache!
You'll never guess, we've got a dog!
She's called Buttons, and she's so
cute. I wish you could see her for
real, but I took a picture of her
when we went to the woods today. We're
only watching her while her owner's
in the hospital, but it feels like
she's ours.
```

Sophie stopped typing, and petted Buttons's soft ears. It was true. Buttons did feel like her dog. "You're the nicest dog I've ever met, do you know that?" she whispered to her, and Buttons turned around and licked her nose lavishly. Sophie giggled, and made *yuck* noises, but really she'd never been happier.

Chapter Six
Good-bye, Buttons

Sophie had made her mom call the hospital every day to see how Mr. Jenkins was, and to pass on messages about how well Buttons was doing. Mr. Jenkins needed an operation on his leg, but he was getting better, and the nurses said he could have visitors. So they suggested that Sophie, Michael, and Tom come, saying that he talked about them all the time and how clever they'd been to rescue him. Mr. Jenkins's son had called the Martins to say how grateful he was to them for taking care of Buttons. He begged them to visit, too, as he wasn't able to stay away from his family in California for very long, and he was worried that his dad was lonely in the hospital.

So on Monday, a week after Mr. Jenkins's accident, Sophie and Tom and their mom knocked on the door of Mr. Jenkins's room. Luckily it was on the ground floor, as Michael was still outside—with Buttons.

Mr. Jenkins was sitting up in bed, reading a newspaper and looking very bored, but he threw it down delightedly when he saw them.

"You came to see me!" he exclaimed. "Is Buttons all right?" he asked eagerly, and Sophie and Tom grinned at each other. Mom had checked with the nurses, and they'd said it was fine to move his bed to the window.

"We've got a surprise!" Sophie explained, as she helped to push the bed to the window. "Look!"

Just outside the window was Michael. Except they couldn't really see him, because he was holding Buttons up in front of his face. She wriggled and woofed delightedly as soon as she saw her owner, and tried to lick the glass.

"Oh, I wish we could bring her in," Sophie said sadly. "She's so happy to see you."

"You've taken care of her so well," Mr. Jenkins said, smiling. "I can't wait to be out of this place and have her back home with me."

Sophie nodded and smiled, but his words made her feel sick. How could she go back to only seeing Buttons in Mr. Jenkins's yard? She couldn't bear it, after having Buttons almost for her own.

Sophie had known all along that Buttons would have to go home again. But the gorgeous puppy felt like a part of the family now. It was going to be so hard to give her up. She could tell from looking at Mr. Jenkins how happy he was to see Buttons. The little dog was all the company he had, now that his family had moved away. But Sophie needed Buttons, too. And Buttons needed owners who could give her all the exercise a bouncy young dog had to have. It was so hard.

Sophie was silent all the way home, and then she took Buttons up to her room (she wasn't supposed to be on the bed, but Mom pretended not to notice the hairs). Sophie petted the puppy's velvety ears, and sighed.

Buttons looked at Sophie, her head to one side, her dark eyes sparkling. She gave a hopeful little bark, and nudged her rubber bone toward her. Sometimes they played a really good game where Sophie pretended to pull the bone away, and Buttons pretended to do fierce growling. But maybe Sophie didn't want to play that today.

Sophie tickled her under the chin, and Buttons closed her eyes and whined with pleasure. Sophie knew just where to scratch.

Sophie sniffed back tears. "I can't give you back," she whispered. "I just can't." But she knew she would have to soon.

"Do you really think we can?" Sophie asked excitedly.

Tom nodded. "I think so. She's so good now. We've been training her to walk, to heel, and stay for almost a month. Anyway, the field isn't too busy today, so hopefully she won't run off and see any other dogs."

"And we've worn her out already," Michael pointed out.

"Okay then." Sophie knelt down next to Buttons, who was panting happily with her tongue hanging out. It had been a long, hot walk up to the highest point of the field. Sophie's heart started to thump as she unhooked Buttons's leash. How would she react?

Buttons looked around in surprise. Then she gave a pleased little woof, but she didn't make a run for it, as Sophie had dreaded she would. She gazed up at Sophie, checking to see if Sophie had meant to let her off the leash. Then she trotted off a few feet, found an enormous stick, and dragged it back. She dropped it at Tom's feet, and barked pleasingly at him.

"She wants to play fetch!" Sophie exclaimed. "We haven't even taught her that. I told you she was clever!"

"You couldn't find anything smaller?" Tom pretended to complain, but he flung the stick as far as he could, and Buttons chased after it, barking delightedly.

They played fetch for a long time, then went home, tired but happy.

Mom was in the kitchen, stirring her coffee, and looking sad.

"What's wrong?" Sophie asked. She had a horrible feeling she already knew.

Mom smiled. "Oh, it's good news, really. Mr. Jenkins came home from the hospital. He's much better, and he asked if we could bring Buttons home." She waved a hand at the counter, which was piled up with Buttons's bowls, and the toys Sophie and the boys had bought her. "Everything's ready. We just need to put it in her basket."

Sophie slumped into a chair, and Tom and Michael leaned up against the counter, all staring at the sad little pile.

"I can't believe she's going," Michael muttered.

"We just got her to come when she was called. We even let her off the leash today," Tom said flatly.

"I know it's hard, but we always knew she wasn't really our dog...." Mom started. Then she sighed. "No, I can't pretend I won't miss her, too."

Dad came in from the yard. "You told them, then?" he asked, seeing everyone's miserable faces. "I'm sorry, everyone, but I told Mr. Jenkins we'd come by sometime this afternoon."

Sophie's eyes filled with tears, as she watched Dad pick up Buttons's basket and start to pack the dog bowls into it.

Dad put the basket down, and came to give Sophie a hug. "You knew it wasn't permanent, Sophie. And you'll still be able to see her. I'll bet Mr. Jenkins would love for you to visit."

Sophie gulped and nodded, and Buttons nudged her affectionately, licking her hand. She wanted Sophie to cheer up, and come and play in the yard. They could do more of the fetching game, with a ball this time. But Sophie was reaching down to clip her leash back on. Buttons gave her a surprised look. Another walk? Well, that was wonderful, but right now? She was quite tired. She'd been planning to have a good long drink before she did anything else, but her water bowl seemed to have disappeared.

"Come on, Buttons!" Sophie said, trying to sound cheerful. She led the dreary little parade out the front door.

Buttons's tail started to wag delightedly as they walked up the path to Mr. Jenkins's front door.

"See, she's happy to be back," Dad said firmly.

Sophie gulped. She wanted Buttons to be happy, didn't she? It would be horrible if she was upset as well. But all the same…. Didn't Buttons love them? Wouldn't she miss them, too?

Buttons waited for the door to open, her tail swinging back and forth so hard it beat against Sophie's legs. Mr. Jenkins's house! Her old house! She was going to see her old owner.

That was what he was now. Her old

owner. She belonged to Sophie these days, and Michael and Tom. But it would still be good to see him.

When the door opened, she tried to fling herself against Mr. Jenkins's legs, and lick him, but Sophie said, "Down, Buttons! Gently!" and she sat back at once. Of course. She had to be careful with Mr. Jenkins. She padded calmly into the hallway, and let Sophie unclip her leash.

"You've done wonders with her," Mr. Jenkins said admiringly. "She's so much calmer. She's like a different dog. I just can't thank you enough."

"She's been really good," Sophie said, her voice tight. "And it was fun training her."

Mr. Jenkins offered them a drink, but

Dad said no, they didn't want to make work for him when he was only just back. Really he wanted to get Sophie and the boys home before Sophie burst into tears.

Buttons watched in surprise as Dad picked up her basket from the hallway and put it down in Mr. Jenkins's living room. That was her basket. But why was it here? Then at last she understood, and she whimpered, staring up at Sophie.

"You're home now, Buttons," Sophie said in a very small, shaky voice. She was holding back her tears. "You're going to take care of Mr. Jenkins, aren't you?" She crouched down and whispered, "Please don't forget us!" in her ear.

Then they left, and Buttons
stared after them out the window.
She remembered now that it was her
special job to look after her old owner.
But she wished she could go home
with Sophie.

Chapter Seven
A New Dog?

With no Buttons, it felt like there was a hole in the house. She wasn't jumping around while the Martins got ready to go out, begging with her enormous eyes for them to take her, too. She wasn't there barking with delight when they got home again. She wasn't sitting under the table during meals, her nose wedged lovingly on someone's knee, waiting for crumbs or the odd toast crust. She wasn't on Sophie's bed at night, so Sophie could burrow her toes underneath her warm weight. She was gone.

The summer days stretched out emptily with no dog to walk. Everyone moped around the house, until Mom and Dad sat the children down to talk one morning, just a few days after they'd taken Buttons back.

"I know you all miss Buttons," Dad told them gently. "We had her for nearly a month, long enough for it to feel like she was ours. But try and think of it like this. You did such a good job taking care of her, and now she's back where she belongs. Mr. Jenkins needs her—she's all he's got. We're really proud of you, you know. Especially all that hard work you put into training her." He smiled at their mom, and she nodded. "So we were thinking, maybe it's time we let you have a dog of your own." He sat back and looked at them hopefully, but no one said anything. And then Sophie got up from the table and ran out of the room.

"She only wants Buttons," Michael muttered.

Dad nodded sadly. "I guess it might be too soon. But I mean it. You all did well. And you deserve a dog of your own, when you're ready."

That weekend, Dad loaded them into the car, and refused to tell the children where they were going. "It's a secret," he said, smiling at their mom.

They drove through town, and Sophie and Michael and Tom tried to figure out where they were going, but Dad wouldn't say.

All of a sudden, Sophie gasped. "The shelter! We're going to the animal shelter, aren't we?" Her voice shook, and she was choking up as she went on. "Please don't, Dad. I don't want to look at other dogs."

"Hey, come on, Sophie, let's just go and see," Tom said excitedly. "Is she right, Dad? Are we going to the shelter?"

"Yup." Dad pulled up close to a big blue sign that said *Forest Lake Animal Shelter*. "And we're here. Come on, everyone."

"Remember we're just looking at the moment," Mom warned the boys, as she walked in with her arm around Sophie, who was trying not to cry.

"We know!" Michael promised, but he and Tom were racing ahead, eager to see all the dogs they were imagining could be theirs.

"I hope this wasn't a bad idea," Mom muttered.

The shelter was full, and all the dogs looked desperate for new homes. Even though Sophie hated the thought of getting another dog—it would feel like she had forgotten Buttons—she had to read the cards over the cages. And once she knew the dogs' names, and their stories, she couldn't help caring about them a little bit.

"Oh, Sophie, look." Mom was crouching next to the wire front of a cage, gazing at a greyhound whose long legs were spilling out of his basket. "He's beautiful. Not that we could get a greyhound; they need so much exercise. Look at his legs!"

"Actually it says here that older

greyhounds don't like too much exercise. They're quite lazy. His name is Fred and he's looking for a quiet home." Sophie looked at Fred, snoozing happily. "He looks pretty relaxed," she said, giggling.

"Oh, it's nice to see you smile!" Her mom hugged her. "You know, even if you don't want a dog now, I'm sure you will one day. You were so wonderful with Buttons."

"That's because she was wonderful," Sophie whispered, digging her nails into her palms so as not to start crying again. "Sorry, Mom." She sniffed hard, and turned back to Fred. "He does look cute, though," she said bravely.

Michael and Tom wanted about six different dogs each, but on the way home in the car even they had to agree that the perfect dog hadn't been at the shelter this time. "But they said they get new dogs all the time, Dad," Tom pointed out. "Can we go back soon?" Sophie leaned against the window and closed her eyes. She wasn't sure she could bear to go again. All those beautiful dogs, wanting a home and someone to love them. But Sophie just couldn't love another dog. Not yet.

At Mr. Jenkins's house, Buttons was moping, too. She tried not to show it, but it was so hard going back to little short walks. Mr. Jenkins was much, much better since his operation, but he still had a cane, and he couldn't walk fast, or for very long. There were no more fantastic runs in the field. No imaginary rabbit-hunting in the woods. Just slow ambles around the streets. Mr. Jenkins couldn't help noticing that his bouncy puppy had turned into a sad young dog. He was glad she was so well-behaved now—Sophie and her brothers had done wonders with her—but he almost wished that occasionally, she would be her silly, happy little self again.

Buttons was very good. She walked to heel, like Tom and Michael and Sophie had shown her. She wondered if Mr. Jenkins would let her off the leash, so she could fetch, but she supposed he didn't know she could do that now. She never tried to get out of the yard, even though she could have, if she'd wanted. She knew how to open the lock after all. She looked at it sometimes, and wondered about going to see Sophie. But she wasn't supposed to. She didn't belong there anymore.

Chapter Eight
The Big Surprise

Sophie's mom put down the phone and came back to the table, where everyone was finishing lunch.

"Who was that?" Sophie asked.

"It was Mr. Jenkins. He's asked us to come over this afternoon." Mom looked at Sophie, whose face had suddenly crumpled, and Tom and Michael, and said firmly, "I told him of course, we would love to. It will be nice to see him."

Sophie stared at her fruit salad, and knew she couldn't eat anymore. "Please may I leave the table," she muttered. She wasn't sure she could be brave enough to go and see Buttons in her real home. Not when she kept imagining her back here.

Her mom sighed and let Sophie go. She looked worriedly at their dad. "It's going to be especially hard for Sophie to see Buttons. She hasn't been in the yard when we've walked past, and I've been grateful. But I suppose it has to happen sooner or later."

Sophie trailed behind the others as they went to Mr. Jenkins's house, walking as slowly as she could. She was desperate to see Buttons, of course she was. And she felt guilty about not going to visit Mr. Jenkins sooner.

But she hadn't been able to make herself go. It had been two whole weeks, and she was only just starting to miss Buttons a tiny bit less. If she saw her again, Sophie knew it would be worse than before.

Mr. Jenkins answered the door, and there was Buttons, tail wagging furiously, gazing up at Sophie, her black eyes full of love. Sophie looked away. But she made herself look back and smile. She didn't want Buttons to be sad, too.

Mr. Jenkins invited them to sit down while he made tea and got juice. He seemed a lot better, although he still had his cane. Buttons stayed next to him the whole time, so when Mr. Jenkins sat down she sat by him, but she stared at Sophie.

Sophie stared back, sadly.

Buttons edged slightly closer, wriggling on her bottom to where Sophie was sitting next to her mom on the sofa. She wanted to cheer Sophie up. She could try, at least. Inch by inch, she traveled the short distance to the sofa, and leaned her nose lovingly against Sophie's leg.

Sophie petted her, her eyes filling with tears. "Oh, I've really missed you," she whispered to Buttons.

Then she realized that Mr. Jenkins was talking. He sounded very serious.

"I need to ask you all an enormous favor." He looked at Buttons, her head in Sophie's lap, and sighed. "All the time I was in the hospital, I wanted to be at home, back to normal, with my dog. The same as things were before. But since I've been back home, I've realized I wasn't taking care of Buttons well enough before. I can't keep up with her!" He smiled sadly. "It's going to be a huge change—I've always had a dog, always had big dogs—but I'm going to have to give her up. I couldn't even manage to train her properly!"

He looked at Tom and Michael

and Sophie, who were staring back at him wide-eyed. "You three did what I just didn't have the energy to do—turned Buttons into a beautifully behaved dog. Since she's been back with me, she hasn't pulled on her leash, she hasn't barged into me. She's been a treasure. But it isn't fair to her, having to live with an old man. She needs to be able to go racing up to the field. So I've decided. She's going to have to go to the shelter. Unless...."

Sophie gulped.

Mr. Jenkins smiled at her. "Unless you can take her. I mean, keep her. Have her as yours. She's missed you, you know. Every time she goes into the yard, she goes and stands by the back fence. She's listening for you in your yard."

Sophie looked up at her mom, her eyes pleading, and saw that her mom was laughing.

"We'd told the children they could have their own dog, because they'd taken such good care of Buttons. We even went to the shelter to look for one. But we couldn't find one we wanted, because we missed Buttons so much. Of course we'll take her!"

Sophie slipped off the sofa, and hugged Buttons around the neck. "You're coming home with us, Buttons! You're really our dog now!" Then she looked up at Mr. Jenkins. "But won't you miss her?"

Mr. Jenkins nodded. "Of course I will.

But it isn't fair to make her miserable, just to keep me happy."

"I could bring her to see you," Sophie suggested, and Mr. Jenkins smiled gratefully.

They finished their drinks, and Mr. Jenkins found all of Buttons's things for them to take home. He was trying to be cheerful, but Sophie could see he was really upset about giving Buttons away. He was going to be so lonely without her.

Sophie was watching him pet Buttons lovingly as they said good-bye, when it suddenly came to her.

"Oh! I've just had the most wonderful idea! When we went to the shelter, there was a greyhound, a beautiful one, called Fred. The card on his cage said he was quite old, and he wanted a quiet home! That's you!"

Mr. Jenkins frowned thoughtfully as he leaned against the door. "A greyhound.... I've never had a greyhound before. I hadn't thought of going to the shelter, but they do want homes for older dogs, don't they." He smiled. "Do you think you and Buttons would let an old man and an old dog tag along on your walks sometimes, Sophie?"

Buttons looked up at Sophie's glowing face, and Mr. Jenkins's smile, and even though she stood still, her tail waved joyfully. Buttons could see they were happy and she was, too—she was going home.

Available now:

Pet Rescue Adventures

3 stories in 1 book

The Kitten Nobody Wanted and other tales

by HOLLY WEBB

Pet Rescue Adventures

The Kitten Nobody Wanted

by HOLLY WEBB

The Frightened Kitten

HOLLY WEBB

The Stray Kitten

by HOLLY WEBB

Three delightful kitten stories to
treasure in one book, from best-selling
author Holly Webb.

HOLLY WEBB

Holly Webb started out as a children's book editor, and wrote her first series for the publisher she worked for. She has been writing ever since, with more than 100 books to her name. Holly lives in England with her husband, three young sons, and several cats who are always nosing around when she is trying to type on her laptop.

For more information
about Holly Webb visit:

www.holly-webb.com
www.tigertalesbooks.com